Dynamite Express

Sheriff Alec Lawson has come a long way from the Scottish Highlands and work is never slow as he deals with a kidnapped woman from China, moonshine that's sending those who drink it blind and a terrifying incident involving a moving train.

But when a man is found dead out in the wild, Sheriff Lawson starts to wonder if the one and only witness might not be telling him the whole truth as to what really happened and decides to start digging a little deeper. . . .

By the same author

Rocking W
The Paducah War
The Horseshoe Feud
Darrow's Law
Cullen's Quest
San Felipe Guns
Darrow's Word
Hyde's Honour
Navajo Rock
Darrow's Badge
Two-Gun Trouble
Silver Express
The Judas Metal
Darrow's Gamble

Dynamite Express

Gillian F. Taylor

A Black Horse Western

ROBERT HALE · LONDON

ISBN 978-0-7198-1374-0

Robert Hale Limited
Clerkenwell House
Clerkenwell Green
London EC1R 0HT

www.halebooks.com

Typeset by
Derek Doyle & Associates, Shaw Heath
Printed and bound in Great Britain by
CPI Antony Rowe, Chippenham and Eastbourne

CHAPTER ONE

'I reckon as they'll jump us there, where the trail goes uphill,' Sam Liston said in his Kentucky drawl. He didn't seem worried by the prospect of an attack.

Alongside him on the driver's seat of the stagecoach was Alec Lawson. Both men were a little below average height, but while Sam was broad-shouldered, Alec was a more slender build, with small hands. Even so, he handled the three pairs of the team's reins with dexterity.

'Probably, if I've guessed right, and they plan to rob this stage, today,' Alec answered, with the soft tones of the Scottish Highlands still in his voice.

Alec Lawson had emigrated, at the age of six, with his parents to the dark and smoky city of Chicago. The difference was so great that the vision of his homeland remained clear and separate in his childhood memories. He often thought that those distant memories of space, fresh air and wilderness were what prompted his love of the Colorado ranges where he had settled after his ten-year stint in the cavalry.

'You all figured they would, so most likely they will,' Sam reassured him.

'The evidence is pretty strong,' Alec admitted, slowing the six-horse team as they approached a slightly steeper downhill section of trail.

It was a hot, late August afternoon: a good day to be out on the eastern side of the Rockies. The trail mostly followed the course of the South Saint Vrain as it flowed out from the mountains to the plain, but in places it left the side of the bubbling water to follow a route higher up the sides of the valley. Ahead, the trail left the river to cross a long spur of higher ground that extended into the valley floor, right to the riverbank. It was forested with clean-smelling pine, clumps of yellowing aspen and white-barked birch. Attractive though the trees were, they were also perfect cover for a group of stagecoach robbers.

As good as he was with horses, Alec Lawson was not a stagecoach driver by profession. He was the sheriff of Dereham County, and a deputy US Marshal. His three closest Army buddies had all left at the same time and now served as his deputies. There had been two stage-coach robberies in the last twelve weeks, in Dereham County. From questioning of the victims and in the local towns, Alec had established that one member of the gang rode a distinctive sorrel sabino – a reddish horse splashed with white markings on its legs and belly, and a white face.

Two days before, Alec had received a telegram in his Lucasville office from a contact in Ballarat, informing him that the sabino was at the town's livery stable.

Alec had ridden out with his three deputies, and following an agreement previously made with the stagecoach line, had taken over the stage when it made its scheduled stop in Ballarat, en route to Lyons and then Lucasville. The three passengers had been left behind in a hotel at Ballarat: Alec's two other deputies, Karl Firth and Ethan Oldfield, rode inside the coach. If the robbers tried attacking this stagecoach, they would be faced with four armed and experienced fighters.

Alec loosened the reins slightly as they reached the bottom of the steep section, and clucked to the team of horses. He looked down at them with a certain degree of pride as the team responded, the reins feeling alive in his hands. The six-horse team moved smoothly, pulling evenly into their collars. As much as he was enjoying the rare experience of driving a team, he couldn't afford to lose concentration. His brown eyes searched the terrain ahead.

'Fifty cents to whoever sees them first,' Sam said, shifting the shotgun he held loosely across his lap.

'You're only saying that because ye've spotted one,' Alec replied.

'Would I do that?' Sam protested indignantly. His handsome, boyish face wore an expression of hurt surprise.

'Aye,' Alec answered simply.

Sam heaved an exaggerated sigh. 'You're no fun, sometimes.'

Alec wasn't offended: he and Sam had met as new recruits, and had been good friends for the following twelve years. While Alec had achieved the rare peace-time feat of working his way up the ranks from private to captain, Sam had been content to make sergeant, and stay under his friend's command. He was loyal, dependable and resourceful and Alec valued him highly, in spite of his occasionally rather trying sense of humour. Sam also had an outstanding gift for accurate shooting; an ability that Alec was willing to gamble his life on.

Alec felt the familiar tingle of anticipation as the stagecoach began to travel uphill. The leather curtains at the coach's windows were partially down, as though to keep out the sun. They also served to partially conceal the armed lawmen inside. Alec glimpsed a slight movement amongst the trees ahead, something that wasn't in keeping with the movement of leaves in the wind. Sam saw it too.

'Right about now. . . .' he said quietly, his eyes bright with eagerness.

The fast-trotting team took another three, four strides. Alec felt his muscles tightening and forced himself to take a deep breath. Then there was a flurry of movement from either side of the trail as four horsemen burst into view.

'Halt!'

The shout was almost drowned by the crack of a warning bullet fired high over the stagecoach. The leading pair of team horses shied and Alec had his hands full for a few moments as he regained control. The four robbers moved quickly into position, clearly well-practised in their attack. Two remained ahead on the trail as Alec drew the team to a sharp halt. The other two, one riding the chestnut sabino, split to either side of the coach. All four men had bandannas drawn up over their faces, and held pistols.

'Drop the shotgun,' ordered the one pointing his gun at Sam.

Sam obediently released the shotgun with one hand, so he was holding it by the barrels, and let it slide down into the front boot under the seat. As Alec applied the brake, Sam sat back and let his right hand rest casually on the coat piled on the seat beside him.

'Stay still and no one will be hurt,' the outlaw leader warned them.

Alec resisted the urge to turn his head as an outlaw on a dark bay passed along his side of the coach. He could hear the horse pulling up and the quick creak of leather as the rider dismounted. The sabino's rider was doing the same on Sam's side of the coach. Alec and Sam both kept their attention on the armed men facing them. All the same, Alec found himself taking a deep breath as the two dismounted outlaws reached the doors of the stagecoach. There were twin crashes as the doors were kicked open from inside, followed by shouts, cries of pain and the whinny of a startled horse.

'Drop your weapons!' The command was from Karl Firth, inside the stagecoach.

In those first few moments of surprise and confusion, the outlaws covering Alec and Sam both looked away, to see what was happening at the sides of the stage. In that brief moment, Sam snatched up the Colt he'd concealed in the folds of his jacket and shot the outlaw leader. Even as the man covering Alec realized where the shot had come from, and started to realign his gun, Sam had targeted him. Sam's second shot tore into his chest, knocking him back and off his horse. His first target was hunched in his saddle, moaning and cursing as his right arm hung by his side.

'Good work,' Alec said briefly, his hands busy with the reins as he controlled the restless team.

He spared a glance back along his side of the stage-coach. He saw Karl Firth jump down to land next to the sprawled body of another outlaw. The now rider-less bay stood a few feet away, snorting as its ears twitched back and forth. Sam had been looking back along the other side of the coach.

'Ethan's taken care of his,' he announced.

'Then let's get this mess cleared up.'

Tying off the reins, Alec climbed down easily from the stage's box, while Sam jumped down on the other side. It didn't take long to deal with the surprised and defeated outlaws. The two that Ethan and Karl had dealt with were bruised but otherwise unhurt. The one shot in the shoulder had the injury roughly wrapped in a bandage fashioned from a spare shirt in his saddle-bags. The one shot in the chest was in a bad way, with blood bubbling from the wound, and from his mouth.

The outlaw had moaned pitifully for a while, before slipping into unconsciousness. Alec helped Ethan to bandage the wound as best they could, but he sus-pected it was a futile gesture. Sam had shot to put down the men who were threatening them; he hadn't had the time to aim his shots carefully. Alec took no pleasure in killing, but he believed in his duty to protect others. He knew he had the skills to make life safer for the law-abiding and had committed himself to a life where he could use those skills. The dying man had chosen to become a bandit, and in Alec's view, had chosen to accept the associated risks, just as Alec chose to accept the risks of the sheriff's job. As he helped Ethan lift the unconscious man into the stage-coach, Alec felt a quiet satisfaction at knowing that it would be a long time before these outlaws had the chance to hurt anyone again.

The other three outlaws were searched, disarmed and handcuffed before being secured inside the coach. Two of their horses were tied behind, and Ethan and Sam mounted the other two. Sam, unsur-prisingly, chose the vividly marked sabino. He grinned at Alec as the sheriff climbed back up to the box seat, accompanied by his senior deputy, Karl Firth.

'Hey, Alec. Can I keep this one?' Sam called.

'Sure, if ye want to swap it for Calico,' Alec replied. 'I can sell her instead.'

'Aw, can't I have both? Please?' Sam put on a plead-ing expression.

'Maybe if he agrees to do stable duty for all our horses, so we don't have to hire someone,' Karl sug-gested, mock-seriously.

Alec chuckled as he took up the team's reins. 'I'd go with that.'

'I want to ride out on my pretty horses and impress

the ladies,' Sam protested.

'You made quite an impression on the ground last time you fell off,' Ethan said. 'That hole was there for a week.'

'At least I didn't come off because I forgot to tighten my girth,' Sam riposted.

Alec swung the whip over the horses' heads to get the team moving.

'Quit bickering, and let's get back to town before it gets dark,' he ordered.

The stagecoach got under way again, and Sam and Ethan fell in on either side, where they could keep an eye on the prisoners through the windows. Alec relaxed, and enjoyed driving the team as they descended from the mountains and headed for the county jail outside of Lucasville.

They were just a couple of miles outside town, not far from the county jail, when Alec and Karl spotted a man riding fast along the trail towards them. The rider waved at them before disappearing from view as the trail dipped into a fold in the prairie.

'I'd guess we're about to get some more work,' Karl commented.

Alec urged the team to a faster trot. 'I was hoping to get some coffee.'

'Don't say things like that. Now I want coffee.'

'At least I'm not suffering alone,' Alec replied, grinning.

A couple of minutes later, Alec was slowing the team as the rider reached them. The man wore plain woollen trousers and jacket, and low-heeled boots; the lawmen were quick to notice that he didn't wear a gun. His square face was decorated with a flourishing moustache. He reined in his blowing chestnut horse on Karl's side of the coach.

'Sheriff Lawson? I was told you were coming into town this way.' He addressed Karl. 'My partner's been murdered!'

Alec smiled wryly: other people had made the same mistake, and he couldn't blame them. Karl was taller and had aristocratically handsome features inherited from his German ancestors. He had a natural dignity that Alec felt he could never hope to match. He believed himself to be an ordinary-looking man, unaware that his fine, regular features and large, dark eyes were attractive. When relaxed, he looked younger than his real age, but when taking command, no one had any doubt about his authority.

Karl gestured towards Alec and the rider turned his attention towards the sheriff, taking in the shield-shaped badge now pinned to the lapel of his jacket, after being concealed for the trap to catch the bandits.

'Sheriff,' the rider repeated. 'We were attacked. I managed to get away but Haylock was gunned down off his horse.'

'Where?' Alec demanded, every inch the sheriff. 'Do ye know who attacked ye?'

'We were a couple of miles out of Pinewood Springs, south of the west fork of the Little Thompson,' the rider said, gesturing back up the trail towards the mountains. 'Haylock and I were heading towards the town when this rancher appeared and done accused us of being cattle thieves. Just 'cause he owns property, he thinks he's got the right to do that. He drew iron on us. I didn't want to get into a fight, so I started to ride away, but Haylock, he didn't like being accused of something he didn't do, so he stopped and argued with the feller. He was madder than a wet hen, I tell you. I figured if I rode off, Haylock would follow, but next thing I know, I hear shooting. I see Haylock fall off of his horse, and the rancher starts turning my way.' He paused before continuing. 'I don't have no gun. I couldn't have fought him; there was nothing I could do to help,' he said pleadingly. 'I just ran. I . . . I left Haylock.' He ran out of words and fell silent.

'Could be Morpeth's land,' Karl said quietly to Alec.

The sheriff nodded. 'Can ye describe the man who attacked you, or his horse?' he asked. 'An' what's your name?'

The rider smoothed his moustache with his hand, an automatic gesture. 'My name's Ford. The rancher had dark hair, I think. He spoke like he was from back in New England, best I can tell.' Ford paused to think. 'I think his horse had a box and some kind of pointy letter, like an M or an N on its flank.' He finished with a nervous, ingratiating laugh that set Alec's teeth on edge.

Alec knew most of the brands in his county: Morpeth's brand was the Box M. All the same, he exchanged a querying look with Karl.

'I didna think Morpeth was the kind to act like that,' Alec said quietly.

Karl shrugged his shoulders. 'I barely know him.'

14

'Right.' Alec's voice became clear and crisp as he gave orders. 'Ethan, you and I will go look for Haylock.' He looked at his two mounted deputies as he spoke. 'Karl, take the prisoners to the jail and get them sorted out.' Alec handed the reins of the stage-coach team to his friend. 'Sam, you're with Karl; I'll take the sabino. Ethan, we'll take one of the other horses with us, to bring Haylock back on. Ford, please stay with Karl and the stagecoach.'

His men obeyed quickly and efficiently and in just a few minutes, Alec and Ethan were riding back towards the mountains, with a horse in tow. With typical fore-sight, Alec took a lamp from the coach, as it would be getting dark by the time they reached the area where the attack had happened. He knew Karl could deal with the prisoners and would get more details from Ford about the fight. He thought about what they had been told as the horses moved at a steady jog along the trail.

'There's something about Ford I didna' like,' he confessed to Ethan Oldfield.

The deputy looked back at him with a mournful expression. It was the usual expression on his long face, and didn't worry Alec.

'Because Ford abandoned his friend?' Ethan asked.

Alec shook his head. 'If things happened as he said, I don't blame him for running. There wasn't anything he did or said I can put my finger on. He just made my skin crawl, right from the moment he rode up.'

Ethan raised an eyebrow. 'That's not like you.'

Alec shrugged. 'Well, I'm not aiming to be friends

15

with him, just to find out what happened.'

'It'll be too dark to see anything much by the time we find Haylock,' Ethan forecast in typically pessimistic style. 'Assuming we find him,' he added.

'At least Haylock won't set my teeth on edge,' Alec replied cheerfully.

CHAPTER TWO

The light was fading from the sky in a beautiful pink and orange sunset when they found Haylock's body. Alec halted the sabino a short distance away, patting its neck as it obeyed, and studied the ground ahead. The body lay twisted partially on to its left side, and even in the poor light, Alec could see smeared patches of blood on the soil.

'Looks like he moved some, after he got hit,' Ethan commented.

'Yeah. You stay here and keep watch while I go take a closer look.'

Alec dismounted and tied the sabino to a choke cherry bush. Lighting the candle in the lamp, he moved forward carefully, studying the marks on the scuffed ground. It was clear that Haylock had dragged himself a short distance after being shot. There was a patch of dark, dried blood on the blue shirt visible under his jacket, and more around his mouth. Alec followed the drag marks and bloodstains back for some fifteen feet. The trail ended at some boot prints, clear enough in the lamplight.

'It looks like he was standing here when he was shot,' Alec called to Ethan.

'Ford said he heard a shot and then saw Haylock fall off his horse,' Ethan replied.

Alec thought back. 'You're right. We'll have to see if Karl writes it down the same. But look, there are footprints here. They're the same size as Haylock's boots.'

'Maybe after he fell off the horse, he got up, then fell again when he tried to move.' Ethan also dismounted and came to join the sheriff.

Alec moved carefully around, holding the lamp at different heights to change the shadows it cast, in the hope of seeing new detail.

'There's no blood anywhere else,' he said, puzzled. 'There's nothing that looks like someone fell off a horse here. In fact, there's no hoofprints just here.'

Together, Alec and Ethan cast about, finding faint marks that led them back to where Haylock's horse had been.

'It looks like Haylock dismounted here, then walked about thirty feet to over there, where he was shot,' Alec said slowly. The light was fading fast now, making the subtle marks on the ground hard to identify. 'If Ford was scared, and riding away, he could have misremembered what he saw,' he mused.

'Our work would be a heap easier iffen we didn't have to talk to the people that saw what happened,' Ethan remarked dourly.

Alec grinned: like Sam's vanity, Ethan's pessimism was an exaggeration of a natural trait, done to lighten the mood during their demanding work. He dropped the act when things got really difficult.

'Let's have a wee look at Haylock before we load him up,' Alec said.

Alec rolled the body on to its back and pulled the jacket open. There were two bullet wounds, close together on Haylock's chest.

'Pretty close shooting,' Ethan observed.

'Most folks would have to shoot twice, pretty rapidly, an' at close range, to get two shots so close together,' Alec said.

'Anyone can get lucky, shooting a target.'

'Not very lucky for this target,' Alec remarked.

The candle in the lamp flickered, plunging the scene momentarily into darkness. Alec pulled the jacket back together and rose.

'Get a blanket from one of the bedrolls and we'll wrap him up and tote him back to town.'

Ethan went to fetch a blanket from one of the robber's saddles while Alec stood and looked at the body in the yellow candlelight. Something about this didn't seem quite right to him. Maybe it was his irrational dislike of Ford that was affecting his feelings. He hadn't liked Ford's rather whiny voice but that wasn't enough to make his skin crawl. Alec had barely even met the man, and already disliked him. He gave a mental shrug, and turned to help Ethan unfold the blanket as he returned.

It was full dark by the time they finally reached the welcome lights of Lucasville. Alec sent Ethan direct to the sheriff's office, to let the others know they had returned, and took the body himself to the under-taker's. Hancock helped him to carry the wrapped bundle inside and they laid it on one of the scrubbed wooden tables in the mortuary. Together, they opened up the blanket.

'Doan' clean him up tonight,' Alec said. 'I want the doctor to take a look at him.'

'It's kinda late to get a doctor; this one's dead,' the undertaker replied.

Alec shot him an exasperated look. 'I want to know how he died. And I ken he's been shot,' he added quickly. 'I'd like to know what kind of bullet, or bullets, how long it took him to bleed out and any-thing else the doctor can tell me about what happened.'

Hancock shrugged. 'Just so long as I get paid.'

'Mebbe he can pay for himself,' Alec said. He searched the corpse's pockets, finding a notebook and silver pencil, some change, a billfold with notes inside, a small, geologist's hammer and a crumpled paper bag containing a few sticky humbugs. Pressing the items into his own pockets, Alec said farewell to the undertaker and set off back to the sheriff's office.

He was pleased to find the stableman waiting for him. Alec handed over the sabino and the horse that had carried Haylock's body, and went straight into the living quarters at the back of the sheriff's office. The room was warm with oil lamps and the smell of bacon and potatoes on the stove. Alec stretched stiffly and spoke to Karl.

'Did ye get the robbers locked up all right?'

Karl nodded. 'Three live ones taken care of, dead one at the undertaker's; paperwork done.'

'Good.' Alec's mind was ticking over with the thoughts of what else needed to be done. 'I want the doctor to go to Hancock's in the morning, to take a wee look at Haylock's body. Did ye speak to Ford?'

'I got a full account of what happened, and told him to stay in town for the time being. He's staying at a boarding house on Sundown Street.'

'I'll see him myself tomorrow: there's some questions I want to ask him.' Alec stirred himself into action again and headed for the door into the offices at the front of the building.

He only took a couple of paces before Karl was in front of him, staring at him with a stubborn expression on his aristocratic face. Alec halted, slightly puzzled.

'What are you planning to do now?' Karl asked.

Ethan moved round to stand beside him.

Alec looked at them. 'I'm going to read your account of what Ford had to say.'

Both men shook their heads as Sam joined them.

'You're going to eat and rest, Alec,' Karl told him.

Alec frowned. 'I've got work to do.'

His deputies' expressions didn't change.

'There's nothing that won't keep until tomorrow,' Karl said. 'You've been on the go all day.'

'I'm the marshal here,' Alec said, glaring at them. 'And sheriff.'

'We outnumber you,' Ethan said.

'Three to one,' Sam added.

21

'So eat and rest, then you can study reports when you're fresh, not when you're so tired you're swaying where you stand,' Karl finished.

Alec suddenly realized that he was deeply tired. Now he thought about it, the bacon smelt very enticing, and he could smell coffee too. 'This is mutiny,' he said, mustering another glare. 'All right, you win, but only this time.'

Sam returned to the stove as Alec made his way to the table and sat down. A mug of coffee was placed in front of him and he picked it up, inhaling the warm smell gratefully. He let out a deep sigh, and found himself beginning to relax for the first time that day. It felt good.

After a good night's sleep, a hearty breakfast and two mugs of strong, black coffee, Alec was ready to discuss the day's duties with his deputies, and to face an hour of paperwork. After reading Karl's account of catching the stagecoach robbers, he added a few notes of his own, then wrote up his thoughts on Haylock's murder. With that done, he heaved a sigh of relief and glanced towards the window. It was another bright day, one to make the most of before the change of season into fall.

Putting the papers tidily away, Alec rose and automatically donned his gunbelt. Shrugging on his brown jacket, he made his way from his private office into the larger one shared by his three deputies. Only Sam Liston was at his desk; he looked up with a sparkle in his bright eyes as Alec approached.

'Got something fun to do, boss?' he asked, leaning back. 'A brothel to inspect?'

Alec nodded solemnly. 'That's right. A real fancy place up Jamestown way.' As Sam's face brightened, he added, 'I need someone to stay in the office this morning, so with Karl and Ethan out, you just got volunteered.'

Sam made a face. 'Spoilsport.'

Alec nodded. 'That's right. I'll be back in an hour or so.'

Several expressions flickered across Sam's face as he realized that Alec couldn't possibly ride to Jamestown and back in an hour. An indignant look was the last one.

Alec grinned. 'I'm going to see the doctor about Haylock's body, then to talk to Ford.' He waved briefly and left, getting the last word for once.

Alec enjoyed walking through the busy town. Lucasville was built on the edge of the plains, an endless sweep of grassland stretching away to the east that was being turned into agricultural land. To the west rose the towering Rockies, carpeted with trees to be turned into lumber and rich in gold and silver deep beneath the soil.

The little town thrived on the mining and agriculture and was the county seat for Dereham County, Alec's jurisdiction as sheriff. He was also a deputy US State Marshal, but it was the sheriff's shield-shaped badge that was normally pinned to his shirt.

As Alec walked to the doctor's, he passed the local school. It was closed now, as it was the summer vacation, but his steps slowed until he halted outside a hardware store facing the school. The school was where Eileen Wessex worked, a young widow who had moved to Lucasville earlier in the year. Alec liked her immensely, and had taken her on a couple of buggy rides into the mountains, but he hadn't seen her now for over a month. He'd simply been too busy with work, and she was busy in the evenings with town societies. Alec was very aware that she'd been widowed just some eighteen months earlier, and was reluctant to press his attentions on her, especially after he'd had to arrest a local miner for harassing her.

Leaning against the hitching rail, Alec indulged in rare introspection. As an only child, he'd left all other family behind when he and his parents had emigrated to America when he was six. His parents had died in a fire at their home when he was fifteen. Only on joining the Army, at twenty-one, had he found anything to replace his lost family. The structured support of military life and the strong bonds it engendered had suited him. All the same, now approaching his mid-thirties, he found himself wishing more often for a family that was truly his own.

Army life had restricted opportunities for love. Now he was a civilian, but still in a demanding and dangerous job. Alec knew he had the skills to be a good sheriff, and that local families benefited from the work he did. It seemed wrong to leave a job where he could make a real difference to the lives of others, and keep families safe, but he didn't think it was fair to ask a woman to marry him, when his work might well get him killed. Eileen had been widowed once, and Alec didn't wish her to suffer that loss again. He recalled the shattering loss of his parents all too well.

A wagon laden with agricultural implements and crates of hardware drew up in front of him, blocking his view of the school. Alec shook his head, then straightened up and moved on, firmly switching his mind back to business.

His visit to Doctor Alden didn't take long. The doctor had retrieved two .44-40 calibre bullets from Haylock's body. It was a commonly used calibre – Alec and his deputies all preferred it as it could be used in both revolvers and rifles – so the bullets offered little help in narrowing down suspects.

'They were in so deep they were almost out the back,' Alden said with a gloomy relish.

'He must have died pretty quickly?' Alec suggested.

The stout doctor nodded. 'Missed his heart but made a real mess of his lungs. He'd have been breathing blood instead of air.'

Alec didn't dwell on the thought. 'Have ye written a report for me?' he asked.

Alden handed over two pieces of paper. 'A report, and my bill.'

After a look at the bill, Alec folded the papers and tucked them inside his jacket. He thanked the doctor for his assistance and left for the hotel where Ford was staying.

He found Ford in the comfortable parlour, reading the local newspaper and sipping a cup of fragrant tea. Ford folded the paper untidily and ran his fingers through his full moustache, as though cleaning crumbs from it. Alec sat down, and after greetings, Ford got straight to the point. 'Have you arrested Morpeth yet?'

Alec made himself meet Ford's gaze. His unreasonable aversion to the man made him want to avoid direct eye contact if possible, but politeness demanded it.

'I havna' yet,' he answered.

'I should have expected as much!' Ford interrupted, before Alec could explain further. 'He's a taxpayer and a voter here, isn't he? Of course you don't want to upset him. People like me never stand a chance.'

'It's no' that,' Alec replied coldly. 'I havna' had the chance tae go speak to him yet. I'm sheriff of this entire county; I've had other things to do.'

'Of course, of course.' Ford held up his hands in a gesture of apology and gave a nervous laugh that grated on Alec's nerves. 'It's been such a shock you see, poor Haylock getting killed right in front of me. He was a decent man; he didn't deserve to die like that.'

'Not many people do,' Alec replied tartly. He shifted in his chair; he somehow couldn't help feeling that Ford's sympathy for Haylock's death was shallow. Not insincere, just not as deeply felt as his words and expression suggested. No doubt his odd antipathy for the man was affecting his judgement. He extracted a small notebook and pencil from a pocket and flicked through to a fresh page.

'Your full name, please?' he asked when ready.

'Frank Ford. I don't have a permanent address at the moment.' Ford gave another apologetic laugh, as if asking the sheriff to excuse his homeless state.

'I see. So what were you and Haylock doing on Morpeth's land?' Alec asked.

'We were just passing through on our way to Lucasville.'

'Ye were off the trail,' Alec pointed out.

Ford nodded. 'You see, we train horses for races, and we both like to keep a lookout for promising animals. So we cut across country to see animals on the range in case there's one worth buying.'

'Ye didna' have any other horses with you yester-day?'

'No.' Ford shook his head. 'I sold my last horse as a brood mare. We were on the lookout for new stock.'

'So if you were off the trail, looking at stock, do ye reckon that's mebbe why Morpeth took you for rustlers?' Alec suggested.

Ford's face brightened. 'Yes, why yes. That could be it!' He laughed again.

Alec suppressed the urge to grimace at the sound. He took a slow, deep breath, and continued with his questioning. 'So Morpeth rode up to you, and started accusing ye both of being rustlers. Was it Haylock who first answered him?'

Alec gradually got Ford's story. It took a while, as he was writing it down so Ford had to keep pausing to let him catch up. Ford sipped his tea and waited. He never seemed to have to think what he wanted to say

27

next, or forgot what he'd just said, and when Alec read it all back, it seemed very similar to what Ford had told Karl.

'I'll write this up properly and ask you to sign it,' he said, putting away the notebook and pencil.

Ford nodded. 'It happened just the way I told you,' he said, combing his moustache with his fingers. 'It's not right that people like Morpeth can get away with the things they do. I had nothing handed to me; I had a hard start in life and I've had to work for everything. The people in charge just don't know what it's like.'

Alec just grunted by way of reply to the last comment. Ford no doubt believed that lawmen were part of those 'in charge', but Alec didn't feel inclined to reveal his own hardships and losses in sympathy. He couldn't help but notice that Ford had a heavy gold watch chain prominently displayed across his vest. This hotel was one of the best in town, with well-made furniture and patterned carpets. Ford clearly had money enough to live well. Alec also noticed that Ford wore low-heeled boots suitable for walking, rather than the higher heeled boots more commonly worn by people who rode a lot. Then again, if Ford was staying in town today, he might prefer low heels.

'I'll ride out and find Morpeth now,' Alec said, rising from the comfortable chair.

'Take care,' Ford warned anxiously. 'You'd better have a deputy with you: Morpeth's a dangerous man.'

'So am I,' Alec replied, a fraction tartly.

'Of course, of course.' Ford excused himself with a nervous laugh. 'I didn't mean to suggest you couldn't cope. But your life is more valuable than his, so I'd hate for you to be hurt by him.'

Ford's solicitous attitude somehow annoyed Alec even more than his envious comments. He forced out a polite farewell, and left the boarding house swiftly.

CHAPTER THREE

Alec walked back to the sheriff's office, his encounter with Ford dominating his thoughts. He couldn't understand why he had such a strong reaction to the other man's presence. Ford's nervous and apologetic laugh was irritating, and Alec didn't care for the way he blamed other people for his problems. However, Alec had encountered similar traits in others before now without their presence making him as uncomfortable as Ford's did. Alec liked to think of himself as rational, while still listening to his gut instinct about things. His strong reaction to Ford confused him. Was he reacting badly to Ford because he sensed, deep down, there was something wrong about him, or did his dislike of the man's character make him attribute motives that didn't actually exist?

He was still puzzled as he entered the front office, and found Sam Liston studying a new pile of Wanted posters. Alec had his own private office; this larger, public one was shared by his three deputies. Karl's desk was the closest to his office. It was as neatly organized as Alec's own and featured a silver inkwell and pen holder that was brightly polished. On the partition wall behind it was a framed photograph of the four lawmen in their Army uniforms, taken just before they finished their terms of enlistment.

Ethan's desk was opposite, to the right of the door. It featured a calendar with sentimental pictures of young women and an almost empty jar of patent hair cream. The wall beside it held the gun rack, and above it, a noticeboard with some handwritten notes, a couple of circulars and a playing card featuring the jack of diamonds with pencilled-on eye-glasses.

Sam's desk was at the back of the room. It was the untidiest of all, littered with odd papers, and featured a shockingly ugly cast iron inkwell that had dust in its many intricate details. Behind the desk, three colourized pictures of showgirls were loosely pinned to the wall, and rippled with interesting effect when the door was opened.

'Howdy, boss,' Sam greeted the sheriff. 'Did you-all speak to Ford all right?'

'Aye,' Alec answered as he crossed to Sam's desk. 'I didna' get anythin' new from him. I'll have to check my notes against what he told Karl yesterday, but it seems pretty much the same.'

'The man must have a good memory,' Sam commented.

'Could be.' Alec dug his notebook out of his pocket and dropped it on Sam's desk. 'I'd like ye to write up ma notes for me.'

Sam gave Alec a dirty look. 'You're sure just abusing

31

your power as sheriff, aren't you?' he accused. 'Being lazy, an' all.'

Alec nodded cheerfully. 'I sure am. Anything happen while I was out?'

Sam heaved a martyred sigh and moved the note-book to the top of an untidy stack of papers. 'The new Wanted dodgers arrived.'

'I guessed that,' Alec said dryly, indicating the pile Sam had been looking through.

'There's been two applications for licences for saloons, one for a liquor store, one for a gambling hall and two for brothels,' Sam continued. 'A complaint about a grocer in Jamestown selling adulterated flour and another about bad whiskey from a saloon in Golden. The last is a report of mules stolen from a claim on the South Saint Vrain.' He handed a sheaf of notepapers to Alec.

'I'm going out to see Morpeth,' Alec said, glancing through the notes. 'I'll visit the claim while I'm out and find out more about the mules. You're in charge here until Karl gets back with Ethan from dealing with that boundary dispute.'

Sam nodded. 'I'll stay here in the shade, then, with the coffee pot, while you go out and ride for miles over the mountains.' He picked up another Wanted poster and began studying it.

'I'll think of you while I'm out in the sun, enjoying the fresh air,' Alec promised, heading for his own office.

He was there long enough to put the notes away, filing everything in the right place. With the papers taken care of, he headed back through the main office and into the living quarters at the rear of the building. Downstairs was one large room, with open stairs leading up to the four small bedrooms on the floor above. One end of this room held the cookstove, cupboards, and a table and chairs. The other end was the living area. There were four comfortable armchairs gathered around a heating stove. A couple of small tables were handily placed for mugs and books. There was also a rather handsome walnut sideboard, inherited from family by Karl, which held various items. Plain shelves supported a number of books, a checkers set, two decks of cards and a silver trophy that Alec had won in a horse-riding competition in the cavalry.

Alec poured himself a glass of water from the jug stored on top of the cupboard by the cookstove. He gulped it thirstily, then covered the mouth of the jug again with a beaded cloth to keep dust and flies out. Leaving the glass by the jug, he cut a chunk of bread and a piece of cheese, wrapping them neatly in brown paper. It was another hour until midday, and he wasn't ready to eat lunch yet, but would be before he reached Morpeth's ranch, so his lunch would travel with him in his saddle-bags. Taking the package with him, Alec headed for the stables.

Shortly after, Alec was out on the trail and heading back towards the mountains. He let his pale-dun horse warm up at a walk, then pushed it into a steady jog after the first mile. As he rode through the high grassland, Alec let himself relax. It was good to be able to put the demands of his job aside for a while and simply to enjoy the pleasure of riding a good horse through beautiful country. Before joining the Army, he'd worked in a railroad yard for three years. His days had been spent among the locomotives, with the reek of coal, smoke and hot oil. Accidents were common, and he'd witnessed two men crushed to death between cars as they'd been coupling them together. To be out in the beautiful country and fresh air was a constant source of pleasure to him.

Wagons passed him along the trail, laden with bales of hay or piled with logs destined for the town. He waved back to a farming family dressed in their Sunday best for a trip into town, and passed a train of heavily laden mules. It didn't seem long before he'd left the plains behind, following the river through its pass between two steep ridges that guarded the entrance to the valley.

Alec arrived at the Box M in the early afternoon. He didn't bother calling at the ranch house, but dismounted and led his horse around to the yard at the back. As he approached, he heard 'Turkey In The Straw' being whistled vigorously. Following the sound, he found a ruddy-faced, bull-necked man sitting on a bench in front of the barn, cleaning a saddle. The man looked up, saw the badge on Alec's jacket, and broke off the cheerful whistling.

'Good afternoon, Sheriff. Water your horse and turn him into the corral, if you like.'

Alec wasn't planning to stay long, but his horse would welcome a break.

'Are ye Morpeth?' he asked, though he'd noticed

the man spoke with a New England accent.

'I sure am,' the burly ranch owner replied. He went on rubbing saddle soap into the dark leather and began whistling again as Alec saw to his horse.

After watering his horse, Alec untacked the dun and turned it into the empty corral. He watched as the horse lowered itself to the ground, then rolled, its legs kicking in the air as it squirmed about to rub away the sweat and itchiness where the saddle had been. Alec chuckled, amused as always by the undignified sight. Leaving his horse to relax, he joined Morpeth on the bench in the sunshine.

'What kin I do for you, Sheriff?' Morpeth asked.

He didn't seem like a man with a guilty conscience, Alec noted.

'A man was killed on your land yesterday,' he said straightforwardly.

Morpeth frowned. 'Whereabouts?'

'Over by the west fork of the Little Thompson.' Alec gave the rancher a more detailed location.

'I got some good steers over on that part of the range,' Morpeth said indignantly. 'I hope none of them got caught up in any shooting, or scared off the area. I'm aiming to sell them steers next month.'

'Only the man who was killed got hurt,' Alec said dryly. 'And it was just the two shots, so far as I ken.'

Morpeth snorted and began rubbing the saddle vigorously again. 'Do you know who the fellow was that got hisself killed?'

'Name of Haylock,' Alec said, watching for a reaction. Nothing but mild interest showed on the rancher's broad face. 'What where ye doing yesterday afternoon?'

'Me?' Morpeth looked mildly surprised at the question. 'I was looking at my crop fields down in the valley by the river. I wanted to see how much work needs to be done, building fences and breaking sod so I can grow more fodder next year. I was too far away to hear any shooting.'

'Were ye by yoursen'?' Alec asked.

Morpeth nodded. 'The men were out bringing in the range horses ready for the fall round-up next week. We got them in the big corrals behind the yard.' He stared at the sheriff. 'Why are you asking what I was doing?'

'Haylock's partner has accused you of the killing.'

Morpeth flushed a darker red and threw the cloth to the ground. 'The hell he did? I never shot no Haylock. Tell me who this partner is and I'll damn well let him know what I think of folk who go throwing out false accusations.'

'He was pretty spooked by seeing his partner shot.' Alec didn't mention his doubts about Ford's version of what had happened. 'He didn't know who attacked them, but the description he gave was a rough match to you; he specifically mentioned a New England accent and a horse with a Box M brand.'

'Gregg is from Vermont,' Morpeth pointed out, referring to one of his ranch hands. 'But I'm sure he didn't shoot no one yesterday.' He snatched up the cloth and began rubbing the saddle harder than ever.

'Did no one see ye out by your fields?' Alec asked.

Morpeth frowned as he thought, then his face changed. 'I saw one of those damn Mexican sheep herders. I warned him to keep his woollies off my land, or I'd shoot them where they stood.'

'Who was he?'

'I don't know his name. All them Mexicans look alike to me. I couldn't understand anything he said to me; it was all that double Dutch, Mexican lingo.' Morpeth waved the cloth dismissively, sending the smell of saddle soap into the air. 'If they want to come live in America, they should damn well learn to speak American, like you and me.'

'Aye,' said Alec, dryly. He had some silent sympathy for the rancher's last point, though. Many times he'd been faced with instructing new cavalry recruits who understood so little English it was a wonder they'd passed the first interview. 'Can ye describe anything about the man, or his horse?' he added.

Morpeth closed his eyes for a moment as he thought. 'He rode a scrubby sorrel mare with a patch of white on its face,' he recalled, looking at the sheriff. 'He had a sheepskin over his saddle, or the sheepskin was his saddle. I didn't look too close. I was keeping an eye on the dog he had with him. It was as black as a skillet and looked as mean as a rattlesnake.'

'Any idea where he might be camping?'

'Not on my land, else I'll run him off, for sure.'

Alec grunted, and leaned back against the wall of the stable. Morpeth wasn't a person he warmed to, but the rancher didn't provoke the same irrational dislike that Ford raised in him. Morpeth seemed too blunt in

37

his opinions to be much of a liar, and Alec was inclined to believe his story about being elsewhere when Haylock's murder had taken place. Or was it just that his dislike of Ford made him inclined to disbelieve the man? At the moment, it was one man's word against the other, until he could track down the unnamed sheep herder. Even then, the sheep herder might not want to provide an alibi for the rancher who had threatened his flock. Alec sat up again.

'I'll need ye to come into Lucasville and sign a statement of what you've just told me, sometime in the next couple of days.'

Morpeth frowned again. His ruddy face seemed darker than ever. 'I'm starting the fall round-up any time now,' he protested. 'I'm busy.'

'I've got an entire county to look after,' Alec countered. 'Whoever killed Haylock is still loose and I've got to find him as well as keep up with the rest of my work. If I have to come out here again, I'll lose time that could affect the lives of many people. I want to see you in my office tomorrow or the day after.' He gave the order with the same force of authority he'd used to command a full cavalry regiment, backed up with his hard stare.

Morpeth nodded, unwilling to argue further.

Alec relaxed, suddenly looking rather boyish. 'Thank ye for your co-operation.'

The burly rancher blinked. 'Have something to eat before you go, Sheriff,' he said respectfully. 'Cook can fix you a bite of something and I'll see your horse gets a feed too.'

Alec smiled. 'That would be most welcome, thank you.'

An hour or so later, replete with salt pork, beans and coffee, Alec was on his way again. Biscuit appeared to have enjoyed his rest too, as he went eagerly with pricked ears. Alec could stay on the higher ground, and head south-east direct to the South Saint Vrain, which meant largely finding his own trail through the forested country. His other choice was to head back along the valley and drop down a series of banks into Muggins Gulch, then to follow the trail until he could cut across a spur between the gulch and the valley of the South Saint Vrain. The second choice would be easier travelling, aside from the matter of descending the banks, which would be a challenge for both horse and rider.

'We wanna get this call about the stolen mules done so we can get home quick, don't we?' Alec asked his horse, rubbing its neck with his knuckles.

The dun's brown-edged ears flickered back at the sound of his voice. It pulled on the reins and broke into a jog.

'That's right,' Alec agreed, easing the reins and letting the horse step out. 'We've had our rest; let's tackle those banks.'

CHAPTER FOUR

The gentle ride seemed to pass in no time until they were at the mouth of the hanging valley. The creek was a dozen feet away, its soft noise turning to a continuous rumble and splashing as it poured over the edge of the hanging valley into a waterfall. The air smelt pleasantly cool and moist as a fine mist rose around the plunging water. From atop Biscuit, the series of drops into the gulch below were daunting. Alec studied them, letting his horse also have a good look. After a few moments, a dangerous grin spread across his face.

'Come on, boy, let's do it.'

He circled away from the edge, then approached at a steady trot. Biscuit lowered his head, gathered himself together, then obediently jumped down. Alec felt as though he'd left his stomach behind as they dropped to the first bank. He stayed balanced over his horse's withers, his hands light on the reins. Biscuit landed neatly, took one stride forward and launched himself into space again. It was terrifying and exhilarating as they swooped from bank to bank. Drop, stride, drop and stride. Alec used his weight and his hands to help the horse keep its balance through the four jumps. Their speed seemed to increase as momentum carried them onward, but the nimble horse kept his feet.

The last drop landed them on the sloping ground of the gulch. Biscuit skidded slightly as strips of earth tore away beneath his hoofs, but he kept going. They raced on for a few strides, Biscuit snorting at each one. Alec remained in balance with his horse, and gradually brought him back to a trot. As they turned towards the trail, Alec glanced back at the banks, now stretching high above him, and laughed aloud at sheer pleasure in their success. He patted the horse's damp neck.

'Good boy, Biscuit. You'll get a good feed when we get back.'

Biscuit shook his head and strode out willingly, his ears pricked. The grin stayed on Alec's face for some time after. The people who only saw the responsible and dutiful side of their sheriff would have been surprised by his enjoyment of the difficult and frankly risky obstacle. His deputies would have expected nothing less.

The visit to the mining claim was straightforward business. Alec got the information he wanted about the mules, and set out on the last leg of his journey, back to Lucasville. He left the spectacular mountains behind, and reached the easier trail across the high plains back to the town. Alec was still a few miles outside of town when he saw a rapidly moving wagon on the trail ahead of him. It came into view from a dip in the ground, a plume of dust marking its progress up the slope as it raced toward Lucasville. It was a heavily built wagon, drawn by two powerful horses who were lumbering along at a fair canter. It didn't seem to be carrying a load, though Alec could see there was something in the bottom of the wagon bed. There were two men on the seat, the driver waving his whip over the team to encourage them on.

The sight was unusual enough to make Alec nudge his horse into a gallop. He didn't race flat out; he just went fast enough to catch up with the wagon. It didn't take long for Biscuit to catch up with the team and their load. As he got closer, Alec could see a man lying in the wagon bed, wrapped in quilts. The driver heard Biscuit's hoofs on the dry ground, and turned to see who was approaching.

'Sheriff Lawson!' Alec called, turning slightly so the sun caught his badge.

The driver slowed his team to a trot. The blowing horses were lathered with white foam whipped up from their sweat.

'We're taking Kershaw to the doctor,' the driver said, as Alec caught up with them. 'He's took real bad all of a sudden.'

Alec glanced at the patient in the wagon bed. He was moaning in pain but only seemed half-conscious. The sides of the wagon were marked with the name of the Little Rose Mine, which was near Lyons.

'Do ye ken the doctor's address?' Alec asked. The two men had a rough idea, so Alec described the street and house for them as he rode alongside the wagon. 'I'll ride on an' let him know you're coming,' he offered.

'Thanks, Sheriff. That's swell,' the driver answered, gratefully. He glanced back at the man in the wagon bed, and shook his team up into a canter again.

Alec was sorry for the tired team, but guessed that they would be well looked-after when their work was done. He legged his own horse into a brisk lope and set off.

Alec found Dr Alden at home and told him about the emergency coming in. The doctor shook his head.

'There seems to be a jinx on the mines around Lyons,' he remarked. 'Had a feller in last week, from the Cornucopia, drank himself blind. Had to send him down to Denver.'

Alec recalled some of the hangovers he'd had back in his Army days. 'There were some nights I had that I regretted in the morning, but I don't recall any of the troops needing much help from the post doctor after a good night.'

'He literally drank himself blind,' Alden said with gloomy emphasis. 'He'd had nearly half a bottle of whiskey and went blind a few hours later.'

Alec cringed inwardly at the thought. 'Is he going to get his sight back?'

'He might recover some vision, but even if he does, I doubt he'll ever be able to see clearly again.'

'I've heard tales of bad liquor making people blind,

43

but I always thought it was an exaggeration. What causes it?' Alec asked.

Alden shifted his weight. 'There's often bad chemicals in cheap moonshine; it doesn't get distilled properly. Ethyl alcohol is the chemical that you get in decent drink, the stuff that makes you happy. Methyl alcohol is the stuff that makes you go blind, or downright kills you. It should be drained off when you're distilling, but moonshine producers don't often bother.'

Alec thought for a moment. 'So it was a bottle of moonshine he got from somewhere that made him blind? I hope to hell there isn't much more of the stuff about.'

'He got the bottle somewhere in Lyons,' the doctor told him. 'But I don't know where from exactly.'

'He was from the Cornucopia, you said?' Alec checked. 'Give me his name, and the names of any friends that brought him in, if you know them. I'll try to find out where he got the whiskey.'

'The fellow's name was Havering.' The doctor scribbled the name on a scrap of paper on his desk. 'I didn't catch the names of the people who brought him in.'

'All right, thank you.' Alec took the scrap of paper and put it in his pocketbook. 'I'll leave you to get ready for Kershaw. Let me know if ye hear of any other cases of people being poisoned by this moonshine, would ye?'

Alden nodded. 'It's good for my business, but I don't like to see men being poisoned because some skunk's passing off bad booze as decent stuff. Defrauding a man over his drink just ain't right.'

'Especially if it maims him,' Alec replied tartly, before leaving.

That evening, Dr Alden sent a note to the sheriff's office. The four lawmen were relaxing in their living quarters, each in his own favourite armchair. Karl had a red leather chair that looked as though it belonged in a gentleman's club, as did Karl with his handsome, aristocratic features and well-turned-out clothes. Sam was sprawled untidily across a chair covered in an incongruous floral chintz that clashed horribly with his multi-coloured bandanna. He was shuffling a frayed deck of cards and swinging a leg over the arm of the chair. Ethan was darning a sock, his long face dourer than ever as he concentrated on the work. His chair was a plain wooden rocker, softened by a patch-work comforter.

Alec returned from the office, where he'd collected the hand-delivered note, and curled up in his own chair. It was a high-backed chair which he liked because it protected him from draughts, and he could rest his head against it and relax. He read the note, and cursed softly.

'What is it?' Karl asked, lowering his book.

'Kershaw died. He was the miner brought into town this afternoon,' Alec added by way of explanation.

'Does Alden say what killed him?' Karl asked.

Alec's face became grim. 'He can't be certain yet,

but he reckons it was kidney failure. And Kershaw had been drinking whiskey from Lyons; his friends said it was called Aspen. Bad moonshine can also cause kidney failure, the doc says here.'

Sam shook his head. 'My Uncle Jed made moonshine up in his cabin, but he always made certain-sure to discard the foreshot. He made damn fine whiskey.'

'I guess there's someone in Lyons selling bad whiskey,' said Karl.

'We've got tae find out where the moonshine's being sold, and who's producing it,' Alec said, his voice tight with anger. 'This stuff's nothing but poison.'

'I'll go to Lyons tomorrow and deal with it,' Karl offered.

Alec's first instinct was to refuse the offer and deal with it himself. Karl must have read it in his expression, because he continued.

'Your horse did a lot of work today, Alec. Let Biscuit rest tomorrow: Woodbine is fresher.'

Alec suspected that Karl's concern was really for himself rather than his horse but he had a point. Relaxing in his armchair, Alec felt reluctant to face another long day in the saddle. 'All right. You go ahead and wear out some more saddle leather.'

He glanced at the note from the doctor again, then put it back in its envelope and dropped it on to a low table.

Sam swung his leg off the arm of his chair and sat upright. 'Who's for a game of euchre?' he asked brightly, holding up the deck of cards.

'Not with those cards,' Ethan complained.

'Everyone knows that the one with the crease across the corner is the ten of diamonds, and the six of spades has a coffee stain on the back.'

'We could play blindfolded,' Sam suggested. 'That would make for an interesting game.'

Ethan had finished his darning. With one quick move, he threw the sock at Sam. Sam caught it in mid-air and threw it back. Ethan caught it clumsily and raised his hand.

'Children!' Alec's shout halted Ethan before he could throw again. 'If ye want to play catch, ye can go outside.'

'He started it,' Sam whined, pointing at Ethan. His eyes were bright with mischief.

Alec chuckled and relaxed. 'There's a brand new deck there,' he said, pointing to the shelf.

Sam bounced out from his chair and grabbed the sealed deck. 'We'll beat them this time,' he said to Ethan, who was rising from his chair.

'You say that every time,' Ethan sighed. 'You're as lousy as a prophet as you are at cards.'

Alec grinned at Karl as they also stood up. 'I need a new hairbrush. You reckon I'll be able to buy one with my share of our winnings?'

'I saw a nice tortoiseshell-backed one in Hardy's last week. You should be able to get that,' Karl said. 'I could do with a new pair of gloves, myself.'

As they gathered around the kitchen table, Alec smiled confidently at Sam and Ethan.

Ethan looked nervous. 'I got some more darning to do.'

Alec shook his head. 'We need four to play, so you're playing.'

Ethan shot Sam a dirty look as he sat down. 'If I lose more than five dollars, you're not waking up in the morning.'

Sam nodded. 'Sounds fair.' He broke the seal on the pack. 'Who's cutting first for dealer?'

The next morning, Karl and Sam set off together in the direction of Lyons. Karl was to try and track down the poisonous moonshine. Sam had a longer ride, as his job was to try and find the sheep herder that Morpeth claimed to have encountered while inspecting his fields. A short while later, Ethan left to escort a prison wagon carrying the surviving stagecoach robbers to a court hearing in town.

Alec made himself another mug of strong, black coffee and took it through to his private office. He left the door between his own office and the front office propped open, so he could see anyone entering through the front door into the public part of the building. Taking a swig of the hot coffee, he spread the assorted papers connected with Haylock's death across his desk, and began studying them.

He puzzled over the discrepancy between Ford's description of the events, and what he and Ethan had seen when they'd found Haylock's body. Alec didn't reckon to be an expert tracker, but he was pretty sure he was right in believing that Haylock had been standing on the ground when he'd been shot, not mounted as Ford insisted. It occurred to him that there might be blood on the saddle, if Haylock had been mounted. Alec leaned back in his chair, absently drumming his fingers on the table. Haylock's horse was unaccounted for. Ford had left horse and rider behind when he'd fled, and there had been no sign of a horse when Alec and Ethan had found Haylock's body. He needed to get a description of the horse and then find it.

Alec grimaced at the thought. No one had reported finding a stray horse: it could have been found wandering and been given shelter somewhere, or could still be out on the range. Unless someone found it and came forward to report it, he and his deputies could spend a lot of time and energy searching for it. They would do it, though: quite apart from the horse's value as evidence, Alec knew it would be uncomfortable if it was wandering loose with its saddle and bridle still on and reins probably trailing around its feet.

He turned to the doctor's report, in the hope that it would make things easier to understand. After reading the first few sentences, Alec went to fetch a dictionary and a copy of *Gray's Anatomy* that Ethan had bought by accident at an auction. With the help of the two reference books, he managed to translate Dr Alden's report into something he could follow. The two bullets had struck Haylock close together, and had travelled into his chest at almost the same angle. It seemed logical to assume that Haylock hadn't changed position much between the two shots hitting him. If either Haylock or his killer had moved, the bullets would have travelled in different directions. That didn't fit with Ford's description of Haylock being shot once, then again as he was falling from his saddle.

Something else occurred to Alec. He checked the doctor's report again and established that the bullets had travelled straight and level through Haylock's chest. His killer, therefore, had been at the same height. Ford's statement said that Morpeth had been mounted when he'd opened fire, therefore Haylock must have been mounted too. Alec sighed; he picked up his mug, but found he'd finished his coffee without realizing it. Putting the mug down again, he leaned back in his chair and let himself relax for a few moments, listening to the sounds of the town coming in through the propped-open window to his side.

He heard the excited voice of a small child, and the mother's quieter answers. Wagons rumbled past and a mule brayed long and loud, from somewhere further down the street. The smells of horses and manure filtered in, so common that they were barely noticed in the bustle of daily life. A stronger smell of cheap tobacco suddenly obscured the warmer stable smells, and Alec wrinkled his nose in distaste. He let his mind wander for a few moments, knowing he would soon pick up his pen and start making notes about jobs to be done. As he relaxed for a few precious moments, his peace was interrupted by the front door of the building opening. Frank Ford entered, and looked around. Alec stifled a sigh, and sat up to attend to business again.

CHAPTER FIVE

Alec Lawson stood up. The movement and the scrape of his chair on the floorboards were enough to attract Ford's attention to his office. Alec called for Ford to enter, and sat down again. He forced himself to meet Ford's blue eyes as he greeted him. There was still that quiver of distaste he felt every time he met the man. As Ford removed his hat, Alec couldn't help being pleased to notice that his dull, brown hair was thinning. Alec's own hair was fine but plentiful, with no visible grey among the dark brown as yet. Cheered up by his observation of Ford's hair, Alec managed a smile as he greeted his visitor.

'I'm glad ye've called,' he said. 'I wanted tae get a description from ye of Haylock's horse. I'm presuming that ye didna' get hold of it after the shooting?'

'No, no,' Ford said, combing his moustache with his fingertips. He glanced at his fingers as though he'd excavated something with them, and wiped them on his woollen trousers. 'It was spooked by the shooting, and poor Haylock falling from the saddle, and ran in

51

the opposite direction to the way I was going.'

Horses are herd animals. Alec knew from experience that a horse that lost its rider tended to stick with other horses, especially ones it was familiar with. But as Ford had said, the horse had been spooked and they could behave differently when frightened. He opened his inkwell and picked up his pen.

'Can ye describe Haylock's horse for me? I wish tae find it.'

'Of course, Sheriff. It's a bay and has a star. Somewhere around fifteen hands, I think. Oh, and it had a white sock behind.'

Alec made quick notes on a scrap of paper. 'Mare or gelding?'

Ford thought for a moment, absently stroking his moustache. 'A gelding.'

'Which side was the white sock?'

'I'm afraid I can't remember.' Ford gave one of the ingratiating laughs that Alec found so annoying.

For a man who worked with horses for a living, Ford seemed remarkably unobservant of his partner's horse. 'Does it have a brand?' Alec asked.

Ford shook his head. 'I'm fairly sure it didn't. I'm sorry I can't be any more help,' he said with a pathetic air that jarred Alec's nerves.

'A name?'

Ford frowned for a moment. 'Brownie.'

Alec made a note of the name. He couldn't help thinking that Ford had just invented a name on the spot. He couldn't think why Ford would bother to do so, if he didn't know. Probably his dislike of the man's ways was affecting his judgement.

Ford leaned forward in his chair. 'Have you arrested Morpeth yet?' he asked eagerly.

Alec shook his head. 'No.'

'Couldn't you find him? Has he lit out?' Ford sounded anxious.

'I found him all right,' Alec answered. 'I spoke to him but I havna' arrested him.'

Anger flashed on Ford's face. 'Why not? He murdered Haylock!'

'I dinna have sufficient evidence tae arrest him.'

'You have my eye witness report. I told you he killed Haylock!'

'An' he told me he was somewhere else at the time.'

Ford's body was stiff with anger. 'You only have his word for that.'

'I only have your word that it was him who killed Haylock.' Alec couldn't help feeling pleasure at Ford's annoyance, but was careful to keep his feelings from his face. 'It's your word against his.'

'Was he with someone else at the time?' Ford was almost shouting.

'We're investigating a possible alibi,' Alec said calmly.

Ford collapsed back into his chair. 'I'm sorry, Sheriff. I'm just so upset about what happened; I've not been able to sleep well since.'

Alec bit back a comment about lack of sleep being better than eternal sleep.

'I'm upset about Haylock, of course.' Ford gave an apologetic laugh. 'But I'm also worried because I'm the only witness. Now Morpeth knows you're investigating him, he might come after me.'

'We could put ye into protective custody in the county jail,' Alec suggested, brightening at the thought of Ford being locked away and unable to annoy him.

Ford frowned. 'I don't think that that's necessary.'

Alec inclined his head. 'It was just a suggestion to make ye feel more secure.'

Ford looked mollified. 'Thank you. I'm glad you understand how important it is to me that Morpeth is arrested, and charged with the crime he's committed. He's a dangerous man, and needs to be removed from society.'

Alec gestured at the papers piled across his desk. 'I can assure ye that we're working hard to bring Haylock's killer tae justice.'

'Are you likely to arrest him soon? Morpeth, I mean.'

Alec stared across the desk. 'I can't say when, or if, I'm going to arrest Morpeth. I'm still investigating.'

'It needs to be done, and it's your duty to do so,' Ford insisted.

'I'll carry out my duty as I see fit.' Alec's voice dropped warningly.

Ford seemed to realize that he'd pushed the sheriff as far as was wise. He dropped his gaze. 'I'm sure you know best,' he said placatingly. 'But I would feel so much safer and happier if I knew that Morpeth was behind bars.'

'If I think he's the killer, he'll be arrested,' Alec

promised. 'If not, then ye don't need tae worry about him.'

'Yes, yes, I guess you're right, Sheriff.' Ford gave an apologetic laugh. He rose.

Alec stayed in his chair. 'Thank you for the information on Haylock's horse.'

'You're welcome.' Ford smiled, placed his hat over his thinning hair, and left.

Alec leaned back, sighed and closed his eyes, letting his irritation fade away.

Ethan returned to the office in the early afternoon. Alec joined him in the kitchen as he made himself a cup of coffee.

'How did the hearing go?' Alec asked, perching on the edge of the table.

'All three jailed until the trial,' Ethan answered, his long face brightened by satisfaction. 'Bail's set at a thousand each.'

'Good. Now we've got them locked up, I'll bring in witnesses from the other robberies to take a wee look at them. If we can get evidence they committed the other hold-ups, we can charge them with those too. The longer they're behind bars, the better.' Alec, too, was satisfied with the result of their trap.

Ethan poured steaming coffee into his mug and dumped in a spoonful of sugar. He stirred it briskly, took a sniff of the rich scent, and sighed in happy anticipation. 'That gonna perk ye up?' Alec asked solicitously.

Ethan nodded, his long face almost cheerful for

once. 'I guess it might,' he admitted.

'Good.' Alec stood up straight. 'You can take over in the office while I go out.'

Ethan tore his gaze away from his rocking chair. 'You're a mean boss sometimes, Alec,' he protested, not quite sincerely.

'You don't have to stay; ye can always quit,' Alec pointed out.

Ethan assumed an indignant expression. 'What? And find a job that doesn't involve riding for hours in the rain, getting shot at by no-good scum, writing reports and having to eat your cooking?'

'At least you only eat my cooking every four days or so,' Alec pointed out. 'If you quit and moved out, you'd have to batch somewhere on your own, and eat your own cooking every day.'

Ethan shuddered. 'At least here I get four different kinds of bad cooking to eat. I guess I don't mind sitting in the office after all.'

'You're always good at finding the bright side of things,' Alec said, grinning.

Alec's first call was on the town's marshal, Tom Clark. The two lawmen liked and respected one another, and helped one another out when necessary. Clark was only a few years older than Alec, but his hair was already a shining steel-grey. There was nothing elderly about the way he walked, or his handshake, however. Alec told him about the poisonous alcohol being sold, and warned the marshal that the bootleg liquor could be in Lucasville saloons too. After that, he gave Clark a description of Haylock's missing horse and asked him to keep an eye out for it. They spent a few more minutes discussing local criminal activity, before Alec took his leave.

After visiting the barber for a shave, Alec headed to the grocer's. On his way, he passed a photographer's store. Most of the window was occupied with photographs of traders and family groups. To one side stood a small easel draped with black crepe and displaying a picture of the outlaw killed in the stagecoach ambush, laid out in his coffin. Alec had seen this kind of macabre souvenir before, though he never understood why people bought them. The picture gave him an idea, though, so he entered the store.

The doorbell jangled as he entered, bringing the owner through from the back. The photographer was a broad-shouldered man, who sported a neatly trimmed goatee. He wasn't wearing a jacket, but had a candy-striped vest over a blue shirt.

'Good afternoon, Sheriff,' said Ennis, the photographer. 'How can I help you?'

'I saw the print of the robber in your window,' Alec said, approaching the desk.

'Ah yes,' Ennis said, before Alec could continue. 'The usual price is a dollar each, but I can let you have one for fifty cents, seeing as I wouldn't have the subject to photograph if it wasn't for your good work.'

'I didna' kill him to make a subject for you,' Alec replied tartly.

Ennis didn't look abashed.

'I'd like ye tae take another photograph for me, as sheriff,' Alec went on. 'There was a man killed two days ago and I could use a picture of him to show tae people.'

'I can do that,' Ennis promised.

'I want the picture for tomorrow.'

'I've got a batch of orders in, but I should be able to manage that,' Ennis said thoughtfully, making a show of studying his order book.

'It's a murder investigation,' Alec said firmly, his Scottish accent more pronounced on the word 'murder'. 'I'll pay a fair price, but no more.' His hard look convinced the photographer not to inflate his price.

They negotiated a price and Alec left, pleased with his idea.

That evening, he joined Karl and his fiancée, Renee Winter, at a concert by the Lucasville Musical Society. It was held in a local dance hall, smartened up for the evening. Alec enjoyed the music, but the main draw for him was Eileen Wessex, who played the flute with the Society. His eyes were mostly on her as the concert went on. Three hours later, refreshed by both the music and pleasure in watching Eileen, Alec said goodnight to Karl and Renee, and made his way to the door at the back of the dance hall. A few others were also waiting: friends and relatives of the Musical Society members. Alec lit the small candle lantern he carried, warming the late evening dusk with its golden glow. After a few minutes, the door opened and the performers began to leave. Alec watched them keenly, and was soon rewarded by the sight of Eileen Wessex, wearing a dusty-pink dress trimmed with cream lace, and a neat cream hat over her hair. A bright smile lit up her lovely face as she greeted him.

'Alec! I thought I saw you in the audience but I wasn't sure it was you. Did you enjoy the concert?' Eileen held out her hand and Alec took it briefly.

'Aye,' he answered. 'It was wonderful.'

Eileen laughed. 'We're not that good.'

'May I walk ye home?' Alec asked.

'That would be lovely,' she replied, making his spirits soar.

They walked away from the dance hall, Alec's lantern casting a soft pool of light ahead of them.

'The concert seemed to be a success,' he said, looking at her as they walked.

Eileen was tall for a woman, almost the same height as Alec, as he was a little shorter than average. She nodded in reply to his comment.

'It was sold out. Hopefully, we have raised a lot towards the fund for a civic concert hall. Lucasville needs one for groups like the Musical Society and the Dramatic Society, and for lectures.'

'It's no' right for ye to be performing in a dance hall,' Alec agreed.

Eileen nodded. 'And it would be nice to have somewhere with proper facilities, like decent seating and dressing rooms.'

'Have the committee chosen where it's going tae be yet?' Alec asked.

'The ideal place would be somewhere fairly central, on one of the main streets, but there aren't many available lots, of course,' Eileen told him.

They continued talking about the proposed new hall until they reached Eileen's modest home. When they reached the gate in the little picket fence, they paused.

'Would you like to come in for coffee?' Eileen asked.

Alec smiled. 'That would be lovely.'

Once inside, Eileen lit the lamps in her parlour and drew the flowered curtains.

'It's turning a little chilly, now it's gone dark,' she said. 'Would you mind lighting the stove while I fix coffee?'

'It's no trouble,' Alec told her honestly.

The well-polished stove was all ready; all Alec had to do was apply a match to the kindling. The room had a pleasant smell of polish and flowers, which was soon joined by the rich scent of coffee. Eileen returned a few minutes later, carrying a tray with the coffee things and a plate of biscuits. Alec watched the domestic scene happily as she poured coffee into the delicate, flower-painted cups and served him. He took a biscuit too, enjoying the sweet, buttery taste.

'This is verra good,' he said.

'Thank you. I enjoy baking and have more time for it during the vacation.'

'I wouldna' know how, even if I had the time,' Alec admitted.

'You have a busy and responsible job,' Eileen said. 'I heard there was a man murdered out on the range a couple of days ago?'

'Aye. Name of Haylock.' Alec sipped his coffee.

'Do you have any idea who did it?'

Alec frowned. 'We were told about it by Haylock's partner, Ford. He says he saw the shooting, and would swear on a stack of Bibles that it was a rancher called Morpeth.'

Eileen picked up on his doubt. 'You think Ford's wrong?'

'Morpeth says he was elsewhere, but so far we've only his word for that. What Ethan and I saw on the ground doesna' match what Ford said happened.' Alec didn't hesitate to tell Eileen about his investigations. He trusted her, and knew she wouldn't pass on what he told her. 'Ford was riding away; he could have mistaken what he saw. I . . . I just don't like the man.'

'You sound surprised by that.'

Alec shrugged. 'He's no' done or said anything offensive. He just makes ma skin crawl. If he enters a room, I want tae leave it.' He sighed, and consoled himself with another mouthful of biscuit.

'That's a very strong reaction,' Eileen said, looking at him with some surprise.

Alec just shrugged, still chewing. He finished his mouthful and washed it down with coffee. 'I can say one of the things that makes me uneasy. Ford says that he and Haylock are racehorse trainers, but he couldn't tell me very much about Haylock's horse. I'd expect someone who works with horses tae be more observant of other's people's horses, especially a partner's.'

'There is horse racing out here?' Eileen asked. 'I

61

don't recall hearing about any courses in the area.'

'It's not like horse racing back East,' Alec explained. 'It's a lot less formal, and most places canna' afford a permanent course. Full-time trainers usually only have a horse or two. They set up matches in different towns against local challengers. They make their money through betting on their horses.'

'I see. So Haylock and Ford are local trainers, then?'

Alec thought for a moment. 'I doan' know,' he admitted. 'I've no' heard of them myself. I'll hafta' ask the local trainers it they've heard of them.' He sipped his coffee and mused over the problem. 'Ford told me that they were riding over Morpeth's land to keep an eye out for potential new stock to train.'

'That seems odd,' said Eileen. 'They might find a bargain that way, if they could see potential in a horse that others couldn't. Even so, most people would wonder why someone wanted to buy a particular horse that hadn't been advertised for sale. Most owners would ask a higher price for it, if it seemed special to the buyer.'

'Aye. It seems kind of strange that neither of them have a horse in training. You'd think they'd have one to race while another's being trained.'

'Maybe they're just bad businessmen?' Eileen suggested.

Alec chuckled. 'That could be it.'

The conversation turned to more general topics. They discussed books at first, and following a mention of Robert Louis Stevenson, Alec told Eileen his memories of his childhood in Scotland. Engrossed in conversation, both of them jumped when the china clock on the mantelpiece struck eleven.

'Och, I'd better be going,' Alec exclaimed.

'I had no idea it was so late,' Eileen said. 'The time passed so quickly.'

'It did,' Alec agreed, smiling at her.

They rose: Alec took a paper spill from a pottery holder on the mantelpiece and lit his candle lantern. Eileen led the way back into the hall.

'Thank ye for the coffee,' Alec said. 'I've had a lovely evening.'

'So have I.' Eileen opened the front door and stood aside to let him pass.

Alec stepped through and turned to face her, reluctant to leave too abruptly. She held out her hand to him and he took it, feeling her warm fingers against his own. Eileen smiled at him, then gave a sudden exclamation.

'I meant to ask you: did that knife wound you got from Dench heal up cleanly?'

Reality hit Alec like a bucket of icy water. Eileen was referring to a shallow knife wound across his ribs that she had stitched up for him. It had healed cleanly and thanks to her fine needlework, all he had to show was a narrow pink scar that would gradually fade to white. He had several other scars as reminders of fights he'd survived. Sooner or later, there would probably be a fight that he wouldn't survive. Alec remembered his decision that he couldn't ask any woman, let alone one already widowed, to marry a man with a job as dangerous as his.

He released her hand and took a step backwards. 'It's healed verra well, thank ye.'

Eileen frowned at the more formal tone in his voice. 'I'm glad.'

Alec wanted to step closer again, to smile at her, but he didn't. He stiffened up as he fought down his instincts. 'Goodnight. I hope you enjoy the rest of your vacation.'

Eileen became distant. 'Thank you for walking me home.'

Alec nodded to her, then turned and walked briskly away.

The lawmen's house was dark when Alec reached it. Karl was still out with Renee, and Sam and Ethan were no doubt at a saloon. Alec looked about the room in the gentle light from his lantern, but the room still looked bleak after Eileen's parlour. That room had rugs, pictures, ornaments and the little touches that made it into a real home. The lawmen's room didn't look too different to the bunk rooms that Alec had known in the Army. It lacked whatever it was that made Eileen's house into a home.

Alec sighed, and headed up the stairs to his bedroom.

CHAPTER SIX

Sam hadn't yet managed to find the sheep herder that Morpeth claimed to have met, so was continuing the hunt. Karl had visited friends of the miners poisoned by the moonshine whiskey and had established that the most likely source was a saloon called the Lucky Dollar, in Lyons. Karl and Ethan were both due to appear in court as witnesses in the trial of some rustlers, so Alec rode out to Lyons on his own.

He stuck to the main trail, choosing to conserve his horse's stamina as far as possible. Lyons was set between three red sandstone mountains. Quarries had sprung up, and as Alec approached the town, he was passed by an ox-drawn wagon laden with blocks of the red stone. Lyons was fairly typical of the towns within his territory: new and still rough-hewn around the edges. It did boast a two-storey school building of the local red stone, on a small hill overlooking the town. Alec rode slowly along the dried earth of the main street, looking at the newer buildings. As it was

almost noon, he stopped at the livery barn he preferred to use, and dismounted.

Biscuit heaved a long sigh and shook himself as
Alec winced at his stiff legs and stretched himself. The
barn was stuffy inside, the smell of horses pronounced, but the dimness was pleasant after the glare
of the sun, and the shade was welcome. Alec led his
horse to a box stall, untacked him and fetched a
bucket of water. Biscuit drank gratefully as Alec
rubbed away the sweaty patches where the saddle and
girth had been, then picked out his horse's hoofs.
Leaving the dun to relax with a small feed, Alec went
to find some food for himself.

An hour later, refreshed by his meal and coffee, Alec
got directions to the Lucky Dollar from the server at the
restaurant and set off. The saloon was down a side street
and was a rough construction of logs that Alec had
never seen before. Alec studied the proprietor's name
over the entrance before he opened the screen door
and entered, pausing just inside to let his eyes adjust to
the lower light. The saloon had the most basic fittings,
though it did sport a large painting of a scantily clad
woman behind the bar. Alec noticed that one of her
eyes seemed to be higher than the other, and there was
something odd about the proportions of her legs, but
her generous breasts were depicted with some skill.

Tearing his attention away from the peculiarities of
the model's anatomy, Alec approached the bar. A
lanky young man lounged behind it, playing a game of
tic-tac-toe against himself on the back of a used envelope. His reddish beard failed to entirely conceal his

poor complexion. The bartender straightened up as Alec approached, sharp blue eyes taking in the badge on Alec's jacket.

'What kin I get you, Sheriff?' he drawled.

'The bar owner,' Alec replied.

The young man blinked, then set down his pencil on the bar, and sauntered through a door behind the bar.

Alec looked around as he waited. There were about a dozen customers scattered in small groups at the tables, with a couple of card games going on. Two men were eating meals and one at a table by himself was reading a shabby newspaper laid on the table, his lips moving as his finger followed the lines of print. A bored saloongirl in a faded dress was playing solitaire at another table.

Turning his attention to the bar, Alec studied the bottles on the crude shelf behind it. He quickly spotted half a dozen bottles of the moonshine whiskey, one of them part-used. The door behind the bar opened and the lanky bartender reappeared, followed by the owner, who stepped around the end of the bar to face Alec. He was a little taller than the sheriff, thick-necked and had a face reddened by weather and alcohol.

'Hansen?'

'Yes.' The saloon owner grunted his reply in a surly fashion.

'Sheriff Lawson. First of all, I want ye tae get rid of all the bottles ye have of the Aspen-labelled whiskey. It's got tae be poured away. An' I want to know where ye got it from.'

Hansen's expression darkened and his body tensed. 'Why?'

'That's stuff's poison,' Alec replied, undeterred by the man's manner. 'One man's been blinded by it and another's died.'

'You cain't prove it was my whiskey that did it.'

'I can. And in any case, you've got no licence to sell intoxicating liquors,' Alec told him. 'If ye don't comply right now, I'll fine you on the spot for selling illegally. If ye co-operate, I'll gie ye—'

Hansen simply lashed out with no word of warning.

Alec didn't need a verbal warning; he saw the shift in weight and the change in Hansen's eyes and was moving before the blow landed. He twisted enough that the punch hit his left shoulder and spun him further in the direction he was turning. He put that momentum into his own blow, striking Hansen on the mouth. Blood burst from Hansen's lips but his head barely moved. His left hand piled into Alec's ribs, staggering him back a step.

Hansen followed up fast, swinging with both hands. Alec knocked one blow aside but took another hit to the same part of his ribs. A burst of pain took his breath away for a moment. Hansen had the advantage in reach, weight and strength: Alec had to use his brains, or else the fight would go badly for him. Hansen grinned and drew back his right arm to launch another hefty punch. Alec stepped backwards, twisting again to soften the impact. Hansen had to lean forward to reach him, his arm at full extension.

Just before Hansen made contact, Alec braced himself on his left leg and delivered a stamping kick to the saloonkeeper's stomach with his right foot. Hansen lost his breath in an explosive gasp, his fist scraping across Alec's shoulder as his attack collapsed.

'Surrender!' Alec yelled, as he brought his foot down and regained his balance.

Hansen gasped a breathless curse and threw himself at Alec, grabbing him in a bear hug. Alec very nearly panicked, then Hansen lifted him off the ground as he squeezed. In spite of the pain shooting through his ribs, Alec retained the clear-mindedness that served him so well in combat. Instead of struggling to free his arms, he simply tilted his head forward and bit Hansen's sweaty neck. Hansen screamed, as the taste of salt and blood seeped into Alec's mouth. The unexpected attack made him panic, and throw Alec away from him.

Alec flew backwards, arms and legs flailing. He landed on a chair, which splintered beneath him and ended up in a heap on the floor. He could do nothing but gasp painfully for a few moments. Hansen clapped his hand to his neck, then removed it to stare in disbelief at his bloodied fingers.

'Son of a bitch!' he exclaimed. 'I'll stomp you into the ground, you animal.'

He lunged forward a couple of paces and stopped beside Alec, raising his right foot to stamp down on to Alec's stomach. Still gasping for breath, Alec threw himself into a roll. He rolled towards Hansen, wincing as he rolled on top of the gun holstered against his thigh. He struck against the leg Hansen was standing on, knocking him off balance. Hansen brought his foot down fast, lurching in his efforts to regain his balance. He ended up straddling Alec's prone body.

Before Hansen could make up his mind what to do, Alec brought his legs up and delivered a full-power kick straight to Hansen's groin. Alec wasn't muscular, but years in the saddle had given him a powerful pair of legs. Hansen emitted a howling cry and dropped sideways. He curled up, clutching at himself, sobbing in pain. Alec almost felt sorry for him, but a twinge from his ribs as he moved reduced his sympathy. He climbed to his feet and straightened his clothing.

'You're under arrest.'

Hansen didn't answer coherently: he just whimpered.

Half an hour later, Alec had everything well under control. After arresting Hansen and cuffing him, he took the names and addresses of the witnesses and got brief statements from them. Alec sent them on their way, then closed the saloon and locked the door. He set aside one bottle of the moonshine as evidence, and instructed the lanky bartender to pour the rest into the hole of the backhouse. The bartender wasn't able to tell him anything about the origin of the whiskey. Alec told him to make a list of all the items in the saloon, and counted the money in the till and the safe. Leaving Hansen locked in his own office, Alec called on the other saloons in the town. None of them stocked the poisonous whiskey, but one owner had also been approached by the moonshiners and had turned them down. He gave Alec a vague description of the two men he'd seen. Alec explained the poisonous nature of the whiskey, and asked the saloonkeepers to contact him if anyone tried to sell them Aspen whiskey.

He also took the opportunity to show people the photograph of Haylock's corpse, but no one recognized the dead man. The last horse race in the area had been three weeks ago, and no one matching either Haylock's or Ford's description was remembered. Alec returned to the saloon and collected the list of its contents, adding the value of the money on the premises at the bottom of the page. The saloon and its contents would probably be sold and used to pay any fines Hansen might be given, in addition to his likely jail sentence for assaulting a sheriff.

Alec returned to the livery barn and hired a heavy-legged, sluggish horse to take Hansen back to the jail at Lucasville. The liver chestnut plodded alongside Biscuit as they returned to the saloon: Alec suspected that Hansen would have trouble getting it into a canter, let along getting it to move fast enough to make an escape. Hansen was still walking awkwardly when Alec brought him out to the horse. His face turned darker red as he studied the broad-backed horse waiting for him.

'Get up,' Alec ordered, nudging him in the back.

Hansen made a low, rumbling noise of disapproval, but stepped forward and swung himself clumsily into the saddle, hampered by the handcuffs. He let out a low hiss as he settled in the saddle, his face contorting briefly, but refused to show any more pain than he could help. Alec mounted lightly and was more successful in concealing the twinges of pain from his ribs. Taking up the lead rope to Hansen's horse, he began the journey back to Lucasville.

When Alec got back to his office, he found that Morpeth had come in and signed a statement of his doings on the day of Haylock's murder. The rancher had also brought in Haylock's horse, which he'd found wandering on his land.

'It matches Ford's description and there's assaying things in one of the saddle-bags,' Karl told him. 'But there's no sign of blood on the saddle, or on the horse.'

'It's no' rained since, so it's unlikely that any blood's washed off.' Alec mused. 'O' course, if Haylock came off right after being shot, there wouldna' ha' been much blood got on the horse.'

'You said the tracks showed he was dismounted when he was shot,' Karl said.

'Aye,' Alec agreed. He pencilled a note on one of the sheets of paper on his desk. 'I need tae know more about Haylock, and what he was doing with Ford.'

CHAPTER SEVEN

Alec spoke to everyone local he knew who was interested in horse racing. None of them had heard of
Haylock or Ford, or recognized Haylock from the
photograph that Alec had ordered. After a day and a
half of fruitless searching, he widened his search. As
Alec and his horse had covered many miles just in the
last couple of days, he decided to take the train up to
Narrow, a mining town at the point where the forested
mountains began to rear themselves up to the snowy
peaks of the Continental Divide.

As much as he loved riding, Alec enjoyed the
chance to relax on a comfortable, velvet-covered seat
and watch the spectacular scenery pass the wide
windows. The railroad rose steadily as it wound along
the valleyside between steep, pine-covered walls of
rock. Foamy waterfalls tumbled down in places, one
so close to the wooden trestle carrying the tracks
that its spray faintly misted the windows for a few
moments.

After two hours on the twisting track, they emerged on to the head of a grassy plateau. Before long, the train began to slow, and the engine whistled as they approached the junction town of Dronfield. The narrow-gauge mountain track split here; one branch headed north-west, towards Narrow, the other went southerly, to Nederland. The train drew up at the station in Dronfield with another whistle and an outburst of steam as the engine settled to a slower rhythm, breathing steadily after the pull up the mountains. A few of the passengers gathered their belongings and left the car. Alec left his seat and followed them. He knew that the train took on water here and he would have a few minutes to stretch his legs.

After speaking to the engineer, Alec made quick visits to three of the town's saloons. He got no more information about either Ford or Haylock, and headed back to the train as the locomotive gave a warning whistle. Alec swung himself neatly up the steps to the platform at the rear of the car and returned to his seat.

The next stage of the journey didn't take long, and Alec disembarked in Narrow less than an hour later. Like most of the other towns in his jurisdiction, Narrow was dominated by the mills that surrounded it. There were lumber mills in the valley, and three mining mills clinging to the slopes above the town. The noise they made filled the air and clouds of dark smoke stained the blue sky above. As usual, after the first minute or so, Alec ceased to notice the noise. He began the same round of visiting saloons, asking about Ford and Haylock and showing the photograph.

It was the fourth saloon where he got lucky.

'Yeah, he an' another feller stayed here, one night,' the barkeep said, studying the picture. 'His friend made out as he didn't have much money and was longing for a decent bed, only he couldn't afford a good room and would be grateful for whatever we could manage. I'd a felt sorry for him iffen he hadn't been wearing a decent suit, and had a gold watch in his vest pocket. I'm damn sure he weren't so poor as he claimed an' I didn't care too hard for him trying to wheedle something out of me.'

Alec grunted sympathetically. 'Did they say anything about what they did, or were doing?' he asked.

Disappointingly, the barkeep shook his head. 'Not anything I could be sure of.'

'Did you get any idea?' Alec pressed.

The barkeep tugged thoughtfully at one end of his droopy moustache. 'I reckoned they might be prospectors. That dead feller was talking some about ores. There was something about assaying too,' he added after a moment's reflection.

'Did they say where they were going?' Alec asked, without much hope of a positive answer. Prospectors tended to be very cagey about their movements, in case of claim jumpers. He wasn't surprised when the barkeep shook his head. He thanked the man, and left a dollar tip behind as he left the saloon.

Alec called at the two livery barns in town, without

75

learning anything else. He had time for dinner before the return train, and enjoyed a plate of ham and eggs and then treated himself to a piece of frosted cake. When his train arrived, he settled comfortably in the high-backed seat and reflected on what he had learnt.

He had found a geologist's hammer on Haylock's body, which supported the barkeep's belief that the murdered man had been a prospector. Alec wondered if Haylock had filed for a claim anywhere. He could check with the land registry office in Lucasville, and check Ford as well. He decided to wire the offices in other towns too. Had Haylock been murdered over a claim he'd found, or perhaps he'd tried to jump a claim? Alec wrote down his thoughts in a small notebook, then stowed notebook and pencil in a pocket. Beyond that, there was nothing he could do before he got back to Lucasville. Settling back in his seat, he switched his attention to the scenery outside, and began to relax.

The steady rhythm of the train was soothing, though the car did shudder now and again as it passed over uneven sections of track. As the train twisted along the sides of the valley, Alec could sometimes see the front section as it turned a curve ahead of the car he was in. The polished brass parts of the black and red locomotive gleamed in the late-summer sunlight. Alec admired the engineering achievement of the train, and the way the railroads had speeded up development around the world, but they held no romance for him, as they did for others. He'd grown to loathe his work at the railroad yard:

the heat, the incessant noise and the filth. He'd witnessed many accidents, more than a few of them fatal, and had quit happily as soon as he was old enough to join the cavalry. He'd figured that the risk of dying as a soldier was no higher than on the railroads, and the cavalry had allowed him to indulge his love of horses.

As he looked idly out of the window, Alec suddenly realized that the front section of the train seemed further away than before. His heart jolted as he sat up, pressing his face against the glass to get a better view. A few moments was all it took for him to be certain that the train had broken in two: one of the link-and-pin couplings had snapped, probably on one of the uneven sections of track. The other passengers were still calm, talking, reading or dozing in the sunny warmth. Alec rose and made his way to the front of the car, moving casually in spite of the fear that tingled along his nerves. The locomotive gave four long blasts on the whistle, the traditional warning of a break-in-two. None of the other passengers reacted to the signal but Alec had to hold down the fear that the sound created. He kept his face schooled into a calm mask as he stepped out on to the small platform at the end of the car.

Closing the door after himself, Alec took hold of the iron rails and carefully stepped over the gap between the cars and on to the platform of the car in front. He took a moment to make sure that his hat was on firmly, then climbed the ladder to the roof. The car swayed beneath him as he cautiously stood up and looked around. This car was at the front of the detached section, which consisted of two passenger cars, a goods wagon and the caboose. Just ahead were the locomotive, tender, and another three passenger cars. Going downhill, the loose cars coasted faster than was a truly safe speed for the locomotive ahead, especially on the winding mountain track. The front section had to stay ahead, though. A gap had opened between the two parts of the train when the break occurred and the suddenly loose cars had briefly lost momentum. Now they were catching up as they coasted downhill. If the locomotive slowed to a safer speed, the wooden cars of the rear section would plough into those ahead and all would shatter.

Looking back, Alec saw the brakeman on the roof of the caboose. The warning signal had been heard. With the wind whipping at his clothes, Alec made his way carefully to where the car's brake stuck up from the roof. Each car had its own brake, operated by a wheel set horizontally on a pole. Alec caught hold of the wheel and clung on to it to steady his balance as the train swayed around another corner. The railroad ran along a trestle-topped raised bank that followed the side of the valley. Here, there was a forty-foot drop to the valley floor below. Even the heavy locomotive leaned out as it took the corner. The lighter cars were already swaying so far that Alec was sure that their cliff-side wheels were lifting briefly from the track on the steeper curves. He began to haul on the wheel, to apply the brake.

Further back, the brakeman was doing the same thing on the caboose. Alec tried to watch the brakeman and the cars, knowing how important it was that the cars braked evenly. As he applied the brake, the car behind caught up and banged against the one Alec was on. The jar made him lose his balance and he swayed precariously, hanging on grimly to the brake wheel. Getting his feet under himself again, Alec stood up.

Fir trees clinging to the rocky valley wall whizzed past as the train thundered on down the track. Alec didn't dare look down into the valley below. He seemed very exposed, on the roof of the car with the wind buffeting him. It wasn't his first time on the roof of a speeding train, but that didn't make him feel any better. He didn't have time to think about fear, though: he had to concentrate on the job at hand.

Timing his move with the brakeman, Alec turned the braking wheel again. The iron wheels squealed in protest and the cars battered together. Again, Alec struggled to keep his balance atop the rattling car as it bounced and swayed. As he gathered himself together, a quick glance showed him that the brakeman was turning his wheel again. The distance between the caboose and the rear carriage widened. Alec grimaced as he frantically turned his brakewheel too. If the caboose was slowed too fast, it might break loose from the rest of the cars. Then there would be nothing to slow the cars behind Alec. He'd have to jump from this one to the next in order to slow that one so it wouldn't pile into the first.

The speeding locomotive ahead reached a curve in the track. It heeled outward slightly as it took the corner; the lighter cars behind it swayed perilously. The section of train that Alec was on was beginning to slow at last, the gap between the two sections of train widening. He couldn't see the locomotive ahead as it disappeared round the bend, the passenger cars rocking from side to side. In spite of the noise of the wind and the locomotive, he could still hear screams from the people inside.

Alec turned his brakewheel again. The cars were slowing now, the headlong flight coming under control. He couldn't relax, though; he was waiting to hear the crash of cars toppling off the tracks into the valley below. His heart was pounding as he gave a last turn to his brakewheel. The cars bumped against one another again but he rode out the jolting without losing his balance this time. Alec held on to the brake-wheel as he turned to look ahead. As their section of train rounded the curve, he heard a whistle from the locomotive ahead. For a moment, Alec froze, fearing that the locomotive had toppled from the track. Then as his car rounded the curve, he could both hear and see the hissing of steam as the locomotive cautiously slowed. The fireman was climbing over the bunker, and as Alec watched, he made the jump to the first of the passenger cars. He landed flat, hands and feet scrabbling for holds on the roof. Alec could do nothing but watch as the fireman slid across the roof before the toe of his boot caught against the raised edge. Moving carefully, the fireman climbed to hands and knees and made his way to the brakewheel. Rising to his knees and bracing himself, the fireman turned the brakewheel, hanging on as the cars behind bumped together.

The two sections of train were gradually brought to a halt. Only when all the cars were motionless, and safely on the tracks, did Alec finally relax. He sat down on the roof of the car, suddenly weak. It was a magnificent view, out across the valley to the mountain slopes on the other side. And all the better for being viewed from a standstill.

By the time the train had been repaired, and returned to Lucasville, Alec had recovered his usual energy. Fortunately, no one had been injured worse than a few bruises, though Alec suspected that nerves might take longer to recover. As Alec was leaving the station, he heard his name being called. He turned and saw the chairman of the Northern Colorado Railroad hurrying to catch up with him.

'Sheriff Lawson.' The sturdy businessman reached Alec's side. In spite of his fine suit, he looked more like a labourer than a company owner. His arrival brought the smell of the rich pipe tobacco he smoked. 'I wanted to thank you. The conductor came and told me how you helped save the train.' He seized Alec's hand in his own, much larger one, and shook it vigorously.

'Thank you,' Alec said, tactfully removing his rather squashed fingers. 'I'm grateful I was in the right place and knew what to do.'

81

'You also had the grit to climb up on the roof of the car and do it,' Webb told him. 'Not many folk would do that. You're a fine man, Sheriff Lawson.'

'Thank ye for the compliment, but it's my job tae protect people. An' in any case, if the cars had crashed, I'd have been hurt too.'

'Well, I'm as glad as can be that you were on that train,' Webb said, clapping Alec on the shoulder with sufficient force to make him take a step sideways. 'Any time the Northern Colorado can help you, just ask. You can ride the Northern Colorado for free, from now on. Any time, any place you want to go on my trains for whatever reason. You don't have to pay one cent.'

Alec had acted without thought of reward, but it would have been churlish to reject Webb's offer. 'It's verra generous of ye,' he replied. 'I'll be glad tae accept.'

'It's little enough for all you've done for me. Now I mustn't keep you.' Webb squashed Alec's hand once more by way of farewell, and left.

Alec returned to the sheriff's office, flexing his fingers cautiously now and again to check they still worked. Karl was the only one of his deputies in the building. Alec went straight to his armchair and sat down with a sigh. Karl set about making coffee without immediately asking questions. Only once he'd passed Alec a mug of steaming coffee, and sat down with one himself, did Karl finally ask if he'd learned anything about Haylock.

'Ford lied to me,' Alec said, somewhat tartly, unable to shake of his dislike of the man. 'Haylock was a prospector, not a horse trainer.'

'Makes more sense that a prospector would be wandering off the trail, than a horse trainer looking for new winners,' Karl said.

'It would also explain why none of the local horse dealers have heard of him.' Alec sighed, then took a long sip of the coffee. 'When you've finished that, I want ye tae go out and wire the sheriffs in neighbouring counties, tae see if anyone's reported Haylock, or a prospector, as missing.'

Karl looked puzzled. 'He's not missing. His death was reported to us just after it happened, and we found his body.'

'An' we've only got Ford's word on what happened to him, and so far Ford's been as crooked as a dog's hind leg. Haylock must have known someone other than Ford. I canna work out who's behind his murder unless I know more about him.'

'If Ford's not been telling the truth, maybe it was Ford who killed him?' Karl suggested.

Alec had considered that. 'Then doesna' make sense for him tae come tell us about Haylock being dead. He could have killed Haylock somewhere out on the range and chances are no one would find the body for weeks, if at all. And if he took Haylock's belongings, we'd have one hell of a time finding out who the body was. And Ford would need tae have some reason tae kill Haylock an' I canna see one right now.'

Karl drank more of his coffee.' You'll figure it out,' he said confidently.

Alec rested his head against the back of his chair, suddenly weary. He just hoped that things would work out as well as Karl believed they would.

CHAPTER EIGHT

Later that evening, Alec received a telegram from one of the saloons in Lyons. The saloon owner had been offered a supply of cheap whiskey of a brand he'd never heard of. He'd bought a bottle as a sample, so Alec arranged for it to be delivered to the law office by the next day's stagecoach.

He was in the front office with his deputies when it was delivered.

'Our sheriff's getting ideas now,' Sam remarked, as Alec began to unwind the wrappings from the distinctively shaped parcel. 'Ordering in special bottles of whiskey, instead of buying the same stuff that's good enough for the rest of us.'

'He's a Scot,' Ethan observed. 'They take their whiskey very seriously. They allus reckon as they invented the stuff.'

'We did,' Alec said, pulling away layers of brown paper.

'I thought whiskey was Irish in origin,' Karl said with studied innocence.

'They stole the idea from us.' Alec pulled the bottle free and held it up.

The amber liquid glowed in the autumn sunshine from the window. The printing on the label was clear, though not high quality, and was the same as on the poisonous moonshine sold in the Lucky Dollar.

'They've not even bothered changing the name,' Ethan said, shaking his head in mournful disbelief.

'Probably don't want to spend the money on getting a new plate for their printer,' Sam suggested. 'Or maybe they'd had a whole slew of the Aspen labels printed somewhere, and didn't want to waste them.'

'If they're trying to sell their stuff to other saloons in the same town, they must think that the Lucky Dollar was closed just because it didn't have a licence,' Karl said. 'They haven't realized that you were there because of their whiskey, Alec. If Lyons is their market of choice, they must be based close by.'

Alec nodded. 'It's more than likely.' He took the lid off the bottle and gave the whiskey a cautious sniff. He wrinkled his nose in distaste. 'Och, that's raw stuff. It must be cheap for anyone tae wish tae drink it.'

'Aren't you-all goin' to try some?' Sam asked mischievously.

Alec held the bottle out to him. 'You can if ye wish.'

Sam looked offended. 'Boss, that stuff's poison! You know I'd take a bullet for you, but that's an honourable way to die. Drinking that rat poison?' He gave a theatrical shudder and pushed the bottle away.

Alec laughed, and replaced the lid. 'I'll take this down to the drug store, and ask Haversham tae analyze it. He should be able to tell if it's got the bad alcohols in it.'

Ethan looked gloomy. 'I never thought there was such a thing as bad alcohol.'

Alec visited Haversham first thing the next morning, to get his opinion on the moonshine whiskey. The drugstore had a distinctive aroma, with strong hints of beeswax, menthol and tobacco in the mix. Alec halted by the gleaming mahogany counter, which had displays of breath-freshening sweets and a patent hair oil of the kind that Ethan used. Haversham approached, carrying the bottle of moonshine. He sucked in a long breath through his teeth before speaking.

'Just like you reckoned, Sheriff. This stuff's like to poison an ox.'

Alec took the bottle. 'Thank you. Do ye reckon it would be safe enough tae drink one or two glasses of the stuff?'

Haversham sucked noisily on his teeth again as he thought. 'I'd guess you'd get the granddaddy of all hangovers, but one glass shouldn't do lasting damage.'

'So the fellow who died from it most likely drank a skinful?'

'I'd say so. Though, I wouldn't swear to it in court,' the druggist added hastily. 'You'd be better asking the doctor.'

Alec nodded. 'Thank you. You've been very helpful and I appreciate you getting the job done overnight.'

Haversham nodded. 'I'll send my bill to the sheriff's office.'

'I'll be expecting it.' He turned and made his way out of the drug store.

Alec next called in at the land registry office. He wanted to know if Haylock had registered a claim, but if he had, it wasn't at the Lucasville office. Alec decided to visit Lyons: he could make enquiries at the land registry there, and also call at the saloon that had been offered the moonshine. Ethan had to appear in court as witness in a case, and Karl was overdue for a day off, so Alec left Sam in the office, and went on his own to Lyons.

As he rode, he pondered the puzzle of Haylock's death. His thoughts kept returning to Ford, who had lied to him. What was Ford covering up? Alec didn't consider Morpeth seriously as a suspect, in spite of Ford's accusation. It seemed more likely that Morpeth was simply a convenient target for Ford to blame. Alec's instinct told him that Ford was more likely to be the killer, most likely over a mining claim, but he couldn't think why Ford would have reported the killing, if so. Could Ford be trying to cover up for someone else, someone he wanted to protect? Alec felt he was missing something, but the more he thought, the more elusive the idea was.

By the time he got to Lyons, Alec was no closer to an answer, and had temporarily shelved the problem. He turned his attention instead to the problem of the moonshiners. The Golden Nugget was the saloon that had been offered the Aspen whiskey. It was on the main street, a larger and fancier place than the unlicensed saloon that Alec had closed down. He hitched his horse on the shady side of the street and crossed to enter the saloon. It was coming up to lunchtime, and the saloon was fairly busy. Alec joined the men at the long bar, and succeeded in drawing the attention of one of the two barkeeps. He indicated his badge.

'I want tae speak tae the owner.' He raised his voice to be heard above the babble.

The nearest barkeeper didn't pause from pouring beer from a jug into a glass.

'He's in the stockroom, at the back.'

'All right.' Alec extracted himself from the press of bodies and made his way to the door at the back of the main bar room.

He found the saloon owner unpacking bottles from a crude wooden box. It only took a moment for him to recognize them as the Aspen whiskey moonshine.

'I warned ye not tae sell those,' he said immediately. 'I had the one ye sent me analyzed, an' they're poison.'

'I wasn't going to sell them,' the saloon owner protested. 'I was gonna pour the stuff away. That's why I'm doing this myself, so that staff don't do anything plumb foolish with the stuff.'

Alec relaxed. 'Is that all you got?' There were a dozen bottles in the crate.

The saloon owner nodded, and stopped unpacking to scratch a red spot on his face. 'The sellers came by and asked if I wanted more. I don't really, seeing as how I can't sell it, but I figured that if I refused, they might pack up and quit the area iffen they can't sell their rotgut here. I didn't know you were going to come calling today.'

'You did the right thing,' Alec told him. He watched the saloonkeeper lift another bottle from the crate and was hit by a sudden thought. 'You're unpacking that now; when did you buy it?'

'Oh, just a few minutes ago, if that.'

Alec swore. 'If I hustle, I might track the seller. Can ye describe him and his horse?'

The saloonkeeper picked up on Alec's urgency and spoke quickly. 'Sure. He had a liver chestnut with a white blaze, and carried the crates on a brown mule. I only bought one crate so I guess he's still packing the other. The man had a brown knitted pullover, I remember, and a red bandanna tucked in. Short whiskers, kinda fair.'

'Good. Write that down in as much detail as you can remember, in case I don't catch up with him now.' With that, Alec spun and left.

Before mounting, he stopped to speak to an idler, resting on the sidewalk in a battered chair. The idler had seen the liver chestnut and mule leave a few minutes ago, and pointed vaguely in the direction they'd gone. Alec swung himself in his dun's saddle and rode away at a brisk jog trot.

Skilful trailing led him to the moonshiners' hideout, a rough group of buildings hidden away among the trees. Alec carefully scouted on foot, finding a stable, a cabin and a still in a clearing. Satisfied that he knew the layout, and the likely number of men involved, Alec rode back to Lyons. He remembered to call at the land registry office but again, there was no record of Ford or Haylock registering a claim. He had more luck at the print shop: they had produced the labels for the Aspen whiskey. After ordering the printer not to mention his visit if the moonshiners returned, Alec stopped for a very late lunch, then rode back to his office.

He found a telegram waiting for him; it was from the sheriff of Ouray County. An assayist from the Pretty Boy mine, named Haylock, had gone missing about ten days earlier. Alec handed the telegram to Ethan.

'I knew Ford was lyin' tae me,' he said with disgust. He sighed. 'I wish I could just nip o'er tae Ouray and talk tae people who knew this Haylock. Even if I take the train, it's gonna be two days at best for the round trip.'

Ethan nodded. 'At least. It'll be longer if the train breaks in two, or derails.'

Alec looked at him. 'You're such a fun person tae travel with.'

Ethan heaved an exaggerated sigh. 'I don't mind the travelling. It's all the things that happen along the way, like accidents, delays, bad weather. . . .'

Alec chuckled. 'You shouldn't worry about those things,' he said. 'You'll probably die from tripping on the stairs and breaking your neck right in your own home.'

Ethan gave him a wounded look. 'You sure know how to raise morale, boss.'

Alec clapped him on the shoulder. 'I learnt it from you.'

Alec mailed a photograph of the dead Haylock to the Ouray sheriff, asking for confirmation of identity. That done, he left the post office and headed for Ford's hotel. Once again, he met him in the comfortable parlour. Ford greeted him warmly, as though they were friends. Alec masked his irritation and smiled politely as he sat down. Ford solicitously enquired after the sheriff's health, then began complaining.

'Are you any closer to arresting Morpeth yet?' he asked. 'You see, it's rather eating into my finances, having to stay here in town.' He gave an embarrassed laugh.

'I can recommend ye a decent boarding house,' Alec suggested. He watched the expressions change quickly on Ford's face as he struggled to choose between comfort and seeking pity.

'I guess I could move,' Ford said at last. 'I mean, I really want to help you out, to get justice for poor Haylock, and you need my testimony that it was Morpeth who killed him, don't you? It's very nice here, and the staff have been so good to me, after the shock of seeing Haylock murdered. But if you want me to stay in town, I could move somewhere cheaper.' He nodded. 'Yes, I suppose I should do that.' Ford straightened his shoulders as if to bear up under a heavy weight.

'Good,' Alec said bracingly. 'You'll feel better if you're no' worrying so much about money.' Not wanting to listen to more of Ford's self-pity, he got straight to the point. 'Now, ye didna' tell me the truth about Haylock. He wasna' horse trainer; he was an assayist at the Pretty Boy mine, in Ouray County. Why did you lie to me?'

Ford's eyes widened briefly. He combed his moustache with his fingers before answering.

'I'm afraid you misunderstood me, Sheriff.' He laughed apologetically. 'Haylock didn't train the horses; I did. Haylock bought the horses and I trained them.'

'I see.' More than ever, Alec wanted to visit Ouray and speak to the people who had known Haylock. He had to take Ford's word on Haylock, and he simply didn't trust the man. Or was it just his strong reaction to Ford that made him see things in the worst light? A knot of frustration tightened his stomach.

'So, how did you get to know Haylock?' he asked.

'We met at a horse race in Ridgeway.' Ford said. 'He had a horse there that someone else had trained, but it didn't run very well and he was complaining about it. I could see that the horse wasn't fit; it had a grass belly. So I told him I could get the horse to run better and Haylock figured he might as well let me have a go. I got the horse fit and it ran well the next time, so we started working together.'

Alec couldn't help but feel that if Haylock had been sufficiently interested in racing horses to buy a decent horse, he would surely have been able to spot something like the grass belly of an unfit horse.

'What colour was the horse?' Alec asked.

Ford hesitated for a moment before answering. 'Chestnut.' He gave an apologetic laugh. 'That was a couple of years ago. Haylock sold the horse after it won a couple of times. He liked the fun of finding something cheap, getting it going, and then selling it for a profit, so I've trained half a dozen horses for him.'

Again, Alec couldn't help but feel that Ford had just invented an answer. Most people who were as involved with horses as Ford claimed to be would have given a more detailed description of the horse. Any white markings, or absence of, would have been mentioned, and possibly height, build and temperament. As the horse that had first brought Ford in contact with Haylock, its importance would surely have meant that its memory would have stayed with Ford. What was more, half a dozen horses seemed a lot to buy, train, race and sell in the space of just two years, though Ford could be exaggerating.

Alec sighed. He'd had enough of Ford's ingratiating manner and apologetic laughter. He rose from his chair.

'Thank ye for your time, Mr Ford. I'm glad we got things straightened out.'

Ford rose also. 'I'm glad to help, Sheriff. Haylock was a good man, and I'm keen to see that justice is done. Morpeth really should be behind bars, by now.'

Alec assumed a bland look. 'When I have the evidence, then I'll arrest him.'

'If there's anything I can do to help, please let me know. The man's a murderer and I'm worried that he'll be after me.'

'Stay in town where we can reach you easily,' Alec suggested. He wanted Ford where he could keep an eye on him, and Ford's belief in Morpeth as a threat was a handy tool.

'I'll do that, Sheriff,' Ford promised.

Alec nodded to him, and left, glad to get away from Ford's irritating presence.

CHAPTER NINE

First thing the next morning, Alec and his deputies rode to Lyons to arrest the moonshiners. Alec had drawn a rough plan of the clearing and the buildings, so the others knew the layout. He'd planned their attack thoughtfully, using their skills to best advantage. A couple of miles beyond the town, they stopped in the shelter of some woodland for half an hour, to rest the horses and take a drink. Ethan read a book, while Sam took the chance to stretch out on the grass for a nap. His gentle snores distracted Alec from his thoughts. Alec glanced over at Sam, then looked at Karl, sitting on the ground opposite.

'He's known you what, twelve, thirteen years?' Karl said. 'He can relax because he trusts you.'

Alec pulled at a tuft of grass. 'I know. You all do, and we wouldn't be such a good team if we didn't trust one another.' He sighed.

'But you're the boss, so if anything goes wrong, it's

your fault.'

Alec looked up, surprised. Karl chuckled.

'That's what you think, isn't it, Alec? But you can't be responsible for everything. You can't be directing everything in the middle of a fight, and you're not responsible for what the bad guys do. No one forced Sam, or Ethan or me to take up law work. We do it, and take the risks, because we believe it's worthwhile, the same as you do. We're adults, Alec, and we've chosen to be here.'

Alec smiled ruefully. 'You're right. I'm grateful tae ye for staying with me. I just doan' want tae let ye down.'

'You've never let us down. We know you do your best for us, and no man can do more than that. We're ultimately still responsible for our own actions.'

Alec glanced at Sam. 'There's one of you who's never responsible if he can help it.'

'I heard that,' Sam said, without opening his eyes.

'Good.' Alec bounced to his feet. 'Let's get on and arrest some moonshiners.'

Another mile or so brought them to the clump of silver birch that marked the faint trail to the moonshiners' cabin. Alec led the way and the others followed in single file. He had no difficulty in retracing the route he'd followed the day before. All the same, he was quietly pleased to see the curve of the trail around a cliff face that he remembered. They were close to the moonshiners' cabin now, and he signalled for silence. The only sounds were the soft rustle and thud of the horses' hoofs in the forest floor, and the creaking of their saddles. As Alec got closer to the bend in the trail, Biscuit raised his head and pricked his ears.

Alec halted instantly and had his hand on his gun when a horse's head appeared around the bend. Behind him, his deputies copied his actions. Alec was lifting and aiming his Colt as the rider came into view.

'Halt! It's the law!' Alec shouted.

He barely glimpsed the rider before the man was spinning his horse and racing back the way he'd just come from. Alec closed his legs hard and Biscuit leapt straight into a gallop. The pounding of hoofs behind him reassured Alec that his deputies had acted just as fast. Still holding his pistol, he steadied Biscuit for the sharp turn around the rock face. The horse responded immediately, shortening his stride as he swept round the bend, leaf mould flying from beneath his hoofs. Alec caught a brief glimpse of the fleeing rider as he wove through the dense trees ahead. Sunlight and shade dappled the scene ahead, making it hard to pick a clean target. Alec didn't bother firing, he concentrated on giving chase.

The moonshiner stayed ahead, knowing his way through the trees. When brighter light warned him they were reaching the moonshiners' clearing, Alec signalled again to his men, and they dropped to a blowing halt, still inside the woodland.

'Ethan, Karl, take the left side. Sam, with me. Karl and Sam, stop and cover the front.'

They did not need more detailed instructions. Alec had already planned for this possibility and briefed them. They split into pairs, each pair going a different way around the clearing, staying out of sight within the woodland. Sam only went part of the way, stopping where he could watch the front of the cabin. Karl would be opposite him, hidden on the other side of the clearing. Alec continued on, meeting Ethan on the far side, behind the stables. They dismounted, tying the horses to trees, and made their way cautiously to the edge of the clearing.

Already, shots were being fired at the front of the cabin and there was the crash of glass breaking.

'Drop your weapons and come out with your hands up.' Karl's shout was audible from the other side of the clearing. The answer was a couple of fast shots from inside the cabin.

There was no one in sight by the stables or the still shack.

'Let's hope they're all being kept busy round the front,' Alec said.

Drawing his Colt, he made the short dash to the stable, Ethan close behind. Keeping close to the log wall, he made his way to the corner. From there, he could see the untacked horse the moonshiner had been riding, standing close against the rails of the corral. The moonshiner had simply abandoned it to seek cover in the cabin, and it was snorting anxiously, seeking the company of the horses and mules in the corral. Peering cautiously around the corner, Alec saw the back of the log cabin. There was a small glass window at the end nearer to him, and a door further along.

'Other end,' Alec said quietly.

They retreated along the wall to the back of the stable, then hurried along to the other end. A quick glance confirmed that they would not be visible from the cabin, so Alec led them to the front corner. When he peered round, there was still no one visible at the window. From this end of the stable, the rear door of the cabin was much closer. Alec glanced at Ethan.

'Ready?'

Ethan nodded, his long face sober. 'Right behind you, boss.'

Alec grinned. 'You allus did like tae be in the safest place.'

With his gun held ready, Alec sprinted across to the back of the cabin, Ethan close on his heels.

They flattened themselves against the wall, on either side of the door. Ethan looked at the wooden latch.

'A shot through the fixing should break it, or at least weaken it,' he said quietly.

Alec simply took hold of the latch and tried lifting it a little way. It moved easily.

'Why bother making a lock for your door when you live in a hidden clearing up a mountain?' he asked, speaking just as quietly.

Pulling back the hammer of his Colt, he jerked the latch up and flung the door open.

Alec was through before it had barely opened half way. He was in a long room that ran from the front to the back of the cabin. There were two doors on the partition wall to his right and a small window at the far end. Two men were at the window, firing out through the broken panes.

'Drop your weapons!' Alec yelled, as he dodged round a narrow bunk against the back wall.

The two men spun around. Taken by surprise, one moved in front of the window as he raised his gun. A moment later, he jerked forward as a bullet hit him from behind. The other man fired a quick shot as he turned, making Alec flinch, and dived under the nearby table. Ethan went in the opposite direction to Alec, towards the outer wall. The injured man stayed on his feet, swaying as he loosed a couple of shots towards Ethan. One tore through the deputy's upper arm, making him stagger as the impact knocked him off balance. Alec changed aim and put a bullet into the injured man, which knocked him back and off his feet.

A shot came from under the table, smashing into the bunk behind Alec. He kept moving, sparing time for a glance at Ethan, who was upright with his gun in his hand.

'I'm fine,' Ethan insisted, though his left arm was limp at his side and blood was running down his fingers.

Alec didn't bother arguing. He fired a shot low, under the table, but it just tore into the dirt floor. As he dodged sideways, he holstered his gun. Another shot came from under the table, almost catching his arm as he turned and reached down. Snatching the greasy blanket off the bunk, Alec bundled it roughly in his arms. Ethan fired at the man hiding under the table, distracting his fire, as Alec sprinted forward a couple of paces. He hurled the blanket over the table, knocking over mugs of beer and scattering the playing cards left on the top. It landed unevenly, trailing almost to the floor on the nearest side, and blocking the outlaw's view of the two lawmen.

Ethan and Alec both kept moving, the sound of their bootsteps overlapping to confuse the outlaw, who would no longer see them. They both fired at the hanging blanket, which puckered and shook as the bullets tore through it. There was an exclamation of pain from behind the blanket, but as Alec was about to call for surrender, he was interrupted by a feminine squeal of fear from the front room.

'Don't shoot!' The call from beneath the table was strained. A plain Colt was pushed out from behind the curtain and slid a short way on the packed dirt floor.

Alec looked at Ethan. His friend's face was pale but determined and he gave a firm nod in response to the look.

'Back out where we can see ye,' Alec ordered, walking cautiously forward, his gun at the ready. He wanted to find the woman he'd heard, to help her, but they had to deal with this moonshiner first. 'Cease fire!' Alec bellowed the order through the shattered window. The shots from outside stopped.

There was a shuffling sound and a bearded man emerged behind the table, swaying as he stood up. He clutched at the edge of the table for support, his plaid shirt stained with blood. Alec gestured with his gun for the man to move towards Ethan's side of the room. As the moonshiner shuffled along, Alec moved to the half-open door to the front bedroom. Ethan also moved forward, keeping the injured man covered. Reaching the door, Alec peered cautiously through the gap.

'Don't move, or I'll kill her!'

A fair-haired man with long side whiskers was holding on to a young Chinese woman, his pistol pressed against her black hair. She trembled as she stood beside him, tears leaking silently from her dark eyes. Tiny and delicate, she was like an exotic flower in this wild, rough place. Beyond them, another man was curled on the floor, moaning and whimpering as blood spread out from beneath him.

Taking a deep breath, Alec forced himself to speak calmly. 'You're surrounded. Let her go now and no one else will get hurt.'

The outlaw shook his head. 'Let me go safe, an' she won't get hurt.'

The girl didn't say anything; she just stood with her eyes downcast and hopeless.

Alec took a slow step closer. The outlaw had his thumb on the hammer of his Colt, but it wasn't pulled back. The time needed to cock the gun would only be a second or so, but it couldn't be instant.

'Stand still!' The man's gun hand twitched briefly towards Alec before he pressed the gun against the girl's head again. She trembled, her lips pressed tightly together.

Holding the outlaw's gaze, Alec reached out with his free hand to shove the door fully open. The outlaw tensed, panic showing in his eyes as he felt himself losing control of the situation.

'I said, stand still!' he shouted, though Alec was only a few feet away.

'Who are ye going tae shoot?' Alec asked, as he slowly raised his gun. 'If ye shoot her, there's nothing tae stop me from shooting you. If ye try tae shoot me, ye won't be aiming at her, and the deputy now outside that window can plug ye in the back.' As he spoke, he nodded towards the shattered window behind them.

The outlaw started to turn towards the window, glimpsed the sudden, sharp movement of Alec's gun and turned back, instinctively turning his own gun away from the girl and towards Alec. The sheriff fired first: blood and bone burst from the outlaw's head and the girl screamed. She staggered as the outlaw's body fell away from her and stood, gasping for breath, her dainty face spattered with his blood. Alec swept forward and impulsively put his free arm around her.

'You're all right, miss,' he reassured her. 'We're here to help you.'

She suddenly threw her arms around him and clung to him, her body warm against his. As she sobbed into his jacket, Alec looked over the top of her head to confirm that the man he'd just shot was no threat. Satisfied, he was holstering his gun when Karl appeared at the window. Alec had been bluffing when he'd claimed there had been a deputy there, knowing the outlaw would turn to check. Karl looked through at Alec, and the woman in his arms, and raised an eyebrow.

'Get in and help Ethan,' Alec said rather sharply.

Karl flashed a quick grin, and moved away.

Stifling a sigh, Alec looked down at the girl's glossy, black hair. Unlike Eileen Wessex, this woman was noticeably shorter than him, and seemed to fit against him very nicely. Alec had to resist a sudden urge to stroke the glossy hair reassuringly. Instead, he gently released his hold of her.

'It's all right,' he repeated softly. 'You're safe now.'

She detached herself quickly from him and stood with her eyes cast down demurely.

'Thank you.' She had a thick Chinese accent. 'I most grateful to noble sir.'

'Och, I'm no' noble,' Alec protested automatically. 'I'm Sheriff Lawson.'

She bowed deferentially. 'So sorry, Sheriff Lawson.'

'What's your name?' he asked.

'I am Lily.'

It seemed an appropriate name for this delicate blossom. 'Well, we'll take care of you, Lily,' Alec promised. 'We'll help ye get back tae your family.'

She shook her head, though she kept her eyes to the floor. 'I don't know where family are. Father sold me when I became woman. Men brought me on ship to America and sold me here.'

Alec felt sick; he shook his head. He took a few deep breaths before he spoke.

'Well, I'll find someone who can help you,' he promised. 'No one owns you now; you are free.'

She looked up at him, and tears silently rolled down her blood-splattered face. 'Thank you,' she said, so quietly he could barely hear her. 'Thank you.'

CHAPTER 10

The lawmen began the job of clearing up after the fight. One good look was enough for Alec to know that the badly injured outlaw wouldn't make it. They did their best to make him comfortable, but he was dead within half an hour. Ethan's injury was nasty, but not dangerous. The bullet had torn through the muscle of his upper arm, just below the skin, but had passed clean through and out. He sat on one of the crudely made chairs as the wound was washed and bandaged.

'There's a doctor in Lyons,' Alec said. 'We'll let him stitch it up.'

'Does he have chloroform?' Ethan asked. 'I want chloroform if he's going to stick a needle in me.'

Sam shook his head. 'I swear Ethan only gets hisself shot so often so as he can enjoy some chloroform.'

'You could just buy some from the pharmacy, you know, and save yourself the pain,' Alec told Ethan.

Ethan was indignant. 'I don't enjoy it! Well, not much. I only take it I when need it.'

'Sure you do.' Alec patted him on the shoulder.

The moonshiner who had hidden under the table had his wound bandaged too. The bottles of poisonous whiskey were poured into the hole of the backhouse and Sam enjoyed himself mightily breaking up the still. The bodies were wrapped in blankets and loaded on to the mules and horses. The wounded man was mounted and tied to his saddle: he moaned and complained, but there was no other way of getting him back to the town. Alec had picked out the quietest of the outlaw's horses for Lily. He'd asked her to pack her things, but all she possessed was a spare dress and set of underclothes, as faded and shabby as the ones she was wearing. Alec gently lifted her to the saddle, where she sat clutching the pommel, her skirts bunched around her. He did his best to arrange her skirts to cover as much of her bare legs as possible, noting some old bruises, and smiled to reassure her.

'You'll be fine,' he promised her, mounting his own horse and taking the reins of hers. 'These men will never hurt ye again and none of us will lay a hand on ye.'

She nodded once, and whispered, 'Thank you.'

On the way back to Lyons, Alec talked quietly to her. He sensitively avoided asking her about the moonshiners and her times with them. Instead he talked about the forest they rode through, telling her about the wildlife, and drawing her attention to differing views as they followed the winding trail. At first, she barely responded, keeping her eyes down towards her hands clutching the pommel. Then Lily began to follow his gentle encouragement to look at the views, occasionally stealing a shy glance in Alec's direction. Soon after, the trail passed a clump of bold, red flowers. Kicking his feet clear of the stirrups, Alec swung down, hanging alongside his horse to pick one of the foot-high plants. Biscuit kept walking steadily as Alec gracefully pulled himself back up and found his stirrups again while handing the flower to Lily.

'It's a wood lily,' he explained.

Her face lit up into the first smile he'd seen from her as she took the flower.

'Thank you,' she whispered, looking at him with wonder.

Alec smiled back, happy to please her and moved by the thought that it was probably the first gift she'd ever been given.

They stopped in Lyons, where arrangements were made for the bodies to be taken care of by the undertaker. The costs would be more than covered by the sale of the moonlighters' horses and mules, which went to the local livery barns. Alec then hired a small buckboard and horse. The injured man had been weakened by the ride down from the moonshiners' base and still faced the trip to the county jail, outside Lucasville. Although she hadn't complained, Alec had realized that Lily was suffering too, not being used to riding, and her bare legs had been rubbed sore against the saddle's fenders. An old horse blanket was put in the back for the moonshiner to lie on, while Alec helped Lily up to the seat to sit beside himself.

It was late afternoon by the time they reached

Lucasville. Karl rode his horse up alongside the driver's seat of the buckboard.

'Have you figured out where Miss Lily will stay?' he asked.

Lily looked anxiously at Alec, still clutching the red flower he'd given her.

'I thought I'd take her to the Reverend Brown's house,' Alec replied. 'He surely canna refuse her refuge.'

'There's some decent boarding houses,' Karl suggested.

Alec looked at Lily, so delicate beside him. He shook his head.

'Not yet. I reckon Miss Lily needs some taking care of and Mrs Brown will do that all right. Unless you'd rather stay in a boarding house?' he asked Lily anxiously.

'I do what you say,' she answered quietly. 'You know best.'

Alec hesitated a moment before speaking. 'I think you'd be better with the Browns at first. You need someone to look after you,' he added passionately, 'after the time you've spent being bought and sold and being made to work like an animal.'

'You are very good,' she said to him shyly, with another heart-melting smile.

Alec shook his head. 'I'm just an ordinary, decent man, I hope.'

Lily didn't reply verbally, but her warm look said plenty.

*

The Reverend Brown and his wife were both at home. They lived in a modest frame house, neatly painted with a few carefully tended plants out front. The Reverend greeted Alec politely, then invited them into the parlour. Lily looked around at the pretty, wallpapered room in silent amazement. Mrs Brown was a warm, plump woman, in a crisp dress of cream lawn, scattered with little blue flowers. Lily made a vague attempt to straighten her limp, faded dress and stood looking shyly at the rug.

'Please, be seated.' Reverend Brown gestured towards the sofa.

Lily looked to Alec, who guided her gently to the seat and sat beside her.

'What can I do for you?' Brown asked.

'I'm hoping ye can help poor Lily, here,' Alec explained, leaning forward. 'Me an' my deputies cleared out a nasty little nest of moonshiners that were making poison whiskey, this morning. Lily, here, was being held as their property.' His voice got more indignant. 'She was sold into slavery in China, brought here, and she's been sold from man to man like an animal ever since.'

Mrs Brown gave a gasp of outrage, looking at the girl with sympathy.

'She's free at last,' Alec went on, looking at her and smiling. 'But she's got nothing; no friends or family, no education, no money or decent way tae earn a living. All she's got is the clothes she stands up in.' He looked at the reverend. 'I was hoping that Lily could stay with you for a wee while. She needs a safe place

111

and guidance while she adjusts tae being free.'

Reverend Brown frowned. 'I don't know that I care to have a heathen girl under my roof, especially one who is almost certainly soiled.'

Before Alec could reply, Mrs Brown spoke up.

'I'd love to have her here. It's not her fault she's a heathen, and how is she going to learn about Christ if we turn her away?' she asked her husband pointedly. She went on without waiting for an answer. 'We've got room for you, dear,' she said to Lily. 'I always wanted a daughter, and you sure seem to need some mothering.'

Lily looked at Alec, who smiled reassuringly.

Reverend Brown looked at his wife, eyebrows raised. 'My dear Mrs Brown, are you sure that this is appropriate?'

'What could be more appropriate than giving a poor heathen girl some decent Christian kindness and a safe refuge? As for her past, it wasn't her fault, and didn't Christ forgive Mary Magdalene?'

Alec resisted the temptation to smile at Mrs Brown's spirited defence. The reverend might rule in matters concerning the church, but the home was her domain. Mrs Brown rose and held out a hand to Lily.

'Come on, my dear. I'll show you to your room, then while you're having a nice bath, I'll look out something from the box of clothes we keep for the poor, just for tonight. Tomorrow we'll go get you some decent clothes and the other things you'll be needing.'

Lily glanced again at Alec, who smiled and stood

up, encouraging her to stand too.

'Mrs Brown will take good care of you,' he promised.

'You go away?' she asked him anxiously. 'Not stay with you?'

'No!' Alec answered rather abruptly. He recovered himself and spoke more gently. 'I share a house with three other men; it wouldna' be appropriate for you to live with us. I can come and see you here, if you like. I'm not far away. You stay with Mrs Brown, you'll love being spoiled by her.'

'That's right.' Mrs Brown took Lily's hand and smiled at her.

Alec took out his pocketbook and gave Mrs Brown twenty dollars. 'Please take this tae buy things for Miss Lily. You're doing so much for her an' I'd like tae help.'

'That's very kind of you, Sheriff Lawson,' she replied.

'Thank you,' Lily echoed.

Alec smiled at her, looking at her as though to fix her face in his memory. He took her hand briefly as he said farewell, then followed Reverend Brown to the front door.

'I'm sorry tae spring this on you unexpectedly, Reverend,' Alec said quietly. 'But I couldn't just abandon the poor, wee girl. She's no' a sinner; she was sinned against by the men that bought and sold her.' His eyes flashed with anger as he spoke. 'She deserves a little Christian kindness to help her make a new life.'

The reverend nodded meekly, knowing when he

113

was beaten. 'Yes, if Miss Lily is willing to embrace a decent life, I believe she can be redeemed. I'm sure Mrs Brown can teach her to be useful in the house,' he added thoughtfully.

'That will be good, but Miss Lily's no' tae be anyone's drudge,' Alec said firmly, guessing that the reverend was thinking of Lily as free labour. 'I hope she'll soon find some work that pays her an honest wage.'

'Of course, of course,' the Reverend Brown agreed. 'I assure you we'll take care of her,' he said as he opened the door.

'I'm sure you will,' Alec agreed, though he was thinking more of Mrs Brown, who wanted a daughter. He was sure that Lily would be all right.

The next day was a Sunday, and Alec went to church in the morning. He didn't attend the little church regularly, but he found the service, with its familiar routines, soothing. The church was half-full when he entered. He walked slowly up the aisle, looking for a place to sit, and exchanging polite greetings with a few acquaintances. About a third of the way in, he suddenly spotted Eileen Wessex on one of the pews. As he stopped, she happened to look round, and saw him. She was wearing her pale-green dress trimmed with cream lace, and her stylish cream hat. Her brown eyes warmed as she smiled at him and Alec smiled back.

He was about to move towards her when he was addressed by someone behind him. Turning, he saw Mrs Brown with Lily. The young woman was wearing a clean, flower-patterned dress and a straw poke bonnet over her glossy hair. The whole effect was simple and modest in a way that Alec found charming. After exchanging greetings, he asked Lily how she was.

'Very well, thank you,' she replied softly, making a slight bow.

Mrs Brown smiled at her affectionately. 'She's such a good girl,' she told Alec. 'She's shockingly ignorant, but it's not her fault. No one ever taught her her letters and numbers or how to tell the time. She can't sew decently, and she can't bake or make pastry. The poor dear's got a lot to learn before she can keep house decently.'

'I'm sure there's no one better to teach her,' Alec replied sincerely.

'She's a heathen,' Mrs Brown went on. 'Never set foot inside a church before, but the Reverend Brown said she should attend services. He's teaching her about Jesus at home, so she can be properly baptized in due course.'

'That's good news,' Alec said.

Lily peeped shyly at him, then demurely lowered her gaze. 'Ye've got a whole new life ahead of ye,' Alec told her. 'And friends now, who'll help ye.' His heart went out to this delicate waif, who had missed so much. He wanted to show her beautiful things and to make up for the years she'd spent as a barely valued possession.

The music changed, and they abruptly realized that the service would very soon start. Alec joined Mrs Brown and Lily as they took seats, sitting next to Lily.

She looked at him and smiled. Alec smiled back, unaware of Eileen Wessex watching him, and then turning away to stare down into her hymn book.

CHAPTER ELEVEN

Later that afternoon, Alec had a visitor; it was O'Connell, the owner and editor of the *Lucasville Daily Trumpet*. He asked to talk privately, so they went into Alec's office, a simple, functional room, and sat down either side of his tidy desk. The newspaperman was brawny, with a drooping moustache and weathered skin.

'What kin I do for ye?' Alec asked.

'Well, there's something I figured I should tell you, s-Sheriff.'

Alec hid a smile as O'Connell corrected himself. The newspaperman had been a sergeant in the infantry and tended to revert to military formality when speaking to Alec, a former captain. He had been about to address Alec as 'sir'.

'What is it?' Alec asked.

O'Connell straightened his back and shoulders as though on parade. 'Yesterday, I was offered a bribe to print a piece in my paper,' he reported crisply.

Alec frowned. 'How much?'

'Two hundred dollars. I didn't take it,' O'Connell added quickly. 'I said I'd think about it, rather than put him off immediately, in case you wanted more evidence, or something.'

'Who was it? What did they want?' Alec asked, reaching for a pencil.

'It was Frank Ford, that racehorse trainer,' O'Connell said. 'He wanted me to write a piece about Morpeth.'

Alec scribbled a hasty note. The simple facts didn't convey the surge of irritation he felt, as much at the mere mention of Ford as at what Ford had done. 'What exactly did he want ye tae write?' he growled.

O'Connell sucked his teeth before speaking. 'He told me about how Morpeth had killed his friend, Haylock, and threatened him. He wanted me to cover the story, emphasizing how dangerous Morpeth is. He kept on at it like a dog worrying a rat, sayin' folks needed to be warned.'

'Do ye reckon he wanted ye tae whip up people's opinion against Morpeth?' Alec asked suspiciously.

O'Connell nodded. 'That's how it seemed to me.'

Alec leaned back in his chair and thought. A public outcry against Morpeth would increase the pressure for him to be arrested. It would also prejudice potential jurors against Morpeth when the case came to trial. His instincts told him that Morpeth was not responsible for Haylock's death, but then who was? Dealing with the issue of Morpeth was distracting him from finding the real killer. If Ford was trying to whip up hate mobs, maybe it would be better to take

Morpeth into custody for his own protection. Another part of what O'Connell had told him came to his mind.

'Ye said Ford offered ye two hundred dollars tae print what he wanted?' Alec asked.

'That's right,' O'Connell agreed. 'He even showed me cash dollars, to prove he had it.'

Two hundred dollars was a lot of money: it would be five or more months' pay for most men. Alec thought of Ford's gold watch and the comfortable hotel he was still staying in. For a trainer whom no one had heard of, Ford seemed to have a lot of money. Where was he getting that money?

'Ye did the right thing in coming tae me,' Alec told O'Connell. 'If Ford comes back tae ye, ask him for more money,' he suggested. 'I'd like tae ken how much he's willing tae spend tae get Morpeth in trouble.'

O'Connell agreed and rose, taking Alec's hand in his own broad, hard one to shake it.

'I sure hope this helps you, Sheriff.'

'I think it will,' Alec answered.

He showed the newspaperman out, and returned to his office to think.

He could hear voices from the living quarters – Sam and Ethan playing an argumentative game of snap – but tuned them out. Why had Ford lied about how much money he had, and what he did? Why was he so keen for Morpeth to be arrested? There had to be some connection between them that Alec hadn't found. Alec sighed, and made notes of the questions he needed to answer.

Tapping the pencil against his desk, Alec stared out of the window, watching people and wagons passing. He tried to relax and approach the problem from another angle. After a few minutes, he found himself thinking about the actual murder. Ford and Haylock had been on Morpeth's land: why? Alec still didn't know what Ford's business really was, but he knew Haylock had been an assayist at the Pretty Boy mine, and had been carrying a geologist's hammer. Could Haylock have been prospecting on Morpeth's land? If so, then was Ford also a prospector? Did he have some connection to the Pretty Boy mine too? If he did, then Alec would have a link between the two men and perhaps a reason for them to be on Morpeth's land together.

Alec pondered the implications of this. If Morpeth knew he had gold on his land, and had found the other men searching for it, he could have attacked them to keep his secret safe. Ford would have lied about not being a prospector because he didn't want others searching in the same place. Ford's accusation of Morpeth killing Haylock then became more plausible. On the other hand, if Morpeth knew or suspected of gold on his land, then why hadn't be mined it himself? Alec knew that Haylock hadn't registered any claims, but had Morpeth?

He paused and looked at the notes he had made. A couple of the questions he'd written could be answered quite simply, and once he had those facts, he could untangle more of the puzzle. Alec decided to visit the land office in the morning, then picked up a fresh sheet of paper and began drafting a telegram to the Pretty Boy mine.

'Did you learn anything at the land registry office?' Karl asked, as Alec entered the front office the following morning.

They were the only people in the room, as the other two deputies were out visiting a rancher who had reported stolen cattle. Alec picked up a cup from the corner of Sam's desk, grimaced at the contents, and set it down nearer the centre of the desk. He perched on the corner of the desk, one leg swinging.

'Morpeth hasn't registered a mineral claim on his land; no one else has either.' Alec withdrew an envelope from the pocket of his brown jacket. 'I stopped at the telegraph office on the way back,' he said, taking out the telegram.

Karl leaned back in his chair and waited while Alec read the short message.

'The lyin' bastard!' Alec spat the words out.

'Would that be Ford?' Karl guessed.

'Aye. Ford is no' a horse trainer, he's a geologist.'

'Does he work for the Pretty Boy?' Karl asked.

'He doesna' work for it; he half-owns it!' Alec slid off the desk. 'Ford discovered the lode. He had tae sell shares for the money tae develop it but he still owns half of it. No wonder he's stayin' in the best hotel; he owns half a gold mine.'

'So that's how he knew Haylock,' Karl said. 'Haylock was the assayist at the mine, and Ford as

121

good as owns the mine.'

Alec glanced again at the telegram, then gazed out of the window. 'So, an assayist and a geologist were out together on Morpeth's land. They must have been looking for gold.'

'But the mineral rights belong to Morpeth; he owns the land.'

'So if they find gold, they need to find a way of getting Morpeth off the land, so they can buy it. Or so Ford can buy it,' Alec corrected himself. 'Ford is the one with the money. But I dinna ken that Morpeth would want to sell the land; it would cost a lot tae get him tae sell. But if Morpeth were convicted, or hanged, then the ranch would be up for sale.'

'Ford would buy the land and mineral rights, and start another mine,' Karl concluded. 'What's more, he might not need to sell shares to raise the money, so this one would be all his.'

Alec gave an exasperated sigh. 'I've been coming at this all wrong. I've been trying tae establish if it was Morpeth who killed Haylock, like I was told. I should have been thinking about why Ford was so keen for Morpeth to be arrested.' He paused as a thought occurred to him, then spoke again, his eyes flashing with anger. 'I bet Ford got Haylock to test ore he'd found on Morpeth's land, then murdered him tae stop him from telling anyone about the gold, an' tae frame Morpeth, so he'd be hanged and the land sold.'

'That's ruthless,' Karl said, his usual calm air displaced by shock.

'I bet I'm right,' Alec insisted. He scowled. 'I got tae

find a way o' proving it.'

He made his mind up abruptly. 'I'm goin' tae Ouray. I have tae speak tae people that ken of both Haylock and Ford.' He spun and glanced at the clock on the wall. 'I just got time tae gather my kit an' catch the next train tae Denver.'

Karl rose from his desk. 'I'll go to the station, buy your ticket, and make sure the train waits for you.'

'Thanks.' Alec flashed him a quick smile of gratitude and sprinted for his room, while Karl hurried to the railroad station.

Alec ran for the train, which was puffing impatiently at the station, grabbed his ticket from Karl as he passed him, with a breathless 'Thank you', and threw himself aboard. He found a seat, tossed his leather bag into the rack overhead, and collapsed gratefully against the velvet-covered cushion. Then he had nothing to do but sit and think for the next hour as the train headed south alongside the foothills of the Rockies, until it reached Denver.

With time to think, he realized that the journey he'd decided on so abruptly would take him some three days of hard travel each way: he'd be away from the office and his deputies for about a week. Was he doing the right thing? The law work would be well taken care of, he was sure of that. He and Karl had worked together closely for several years now, and thought very much alike, in spite of the differences in their backgrounds. Sam and Ethan were as loyal to Karl as they were to himself. Alec shook his head, as if to clear it. He was going to Ouray.

First was the change of train at Denver. There, he ate dinner while he waited the two hours for his next train. Alec also sent a telegram to the sheriff of Ouray County, asking to meet him. The new railroad continued south at first. Alec read the copy of the *Rocky Mountain News* that he'd bought in Denver. After another short stop at Colorado Springs, the railroad turned west and headed into the Rockies. At first, Alec enjoyed the change of scenery, but after a while, his thoughts began to turn to Miss Lily. He wondered how she was getting on with the Browns and imagined her in her clean, print dress, cooking and sewing. Alec began to plan trips out, to show her the places he loved in this beautiful country.

His daydreams were broken by a stop at Cañon City. It was late afternoon now, and although Alec was hungry, there was only thirty minutes in which to refresh himself and get a meal. His air of command, and the deputy marshal's badge on his lapel, got him a cup of coffee and a plate of stew in short order. It was a relief to be back on the comparative peace of the train. As time passed, it got darker as the sun sank behind the mountains. When the train crossed the continental divide the cars were lit for a while by the glow of the setting sun. The light came and went as the train wound its way through the peaks but before long, they were travelling in the dark.

Like the passengers around him, Alec squirmed himself around in his seat and tried to sleep as the train continued on through the night. When he did get to sleep, he was woken again by the shriek of the whistle and the jolting as the train stopped at Gunnison. He stumbled out of the train, stiff-legged, for a quick break. The cool, fresh air was welcome after the stuffiness of the train. Alec moved to the end of the platform and looked up at the distant, clear stars for a few minutes, letting his mind relax and clear. When he boarded again, he dozed sporadically in his seat as the train clattered on through the night.

They reached Montrose in the early morning. Yawning, Alec found a restaurant and filled up with ham and eggs, and three mugs of strong, black coffee. Refreshed, he visited the livery stables, and picked out the best horse he could find. With some fresh-baked bread, cheese and a chunk of sausage stowed in the saddle-bags, and his leather bag tied behind the saddle, Alec began the forty-mile ride to Ouray.

It was late afternoon when he arrived. After settling his horse at a livery stable, Alec booked himself a room at a hotel. He looked at the bed longingly, but made himself go in search of Sheriff Bezener. The sheriff of Ouray County was a barrel-shaped man who adorned his face with a droopy moustache. He picked his teeth with a small, ivory pick while Alec talked to him, explaining his reasons for visiting another sheriff's jurisdiction.

'I do recall as someone said this feller from the Pretty Boy had gone missing,' Bezener drawled. He gestured with the toothpick, which had a fragment of meat stuck to the end. Bezener noticed the fragment, sucked it off and swallowed thoughtfully. 'I asked around some, but no one knew where that feller had gone.'

'If they knew, he wouldna' be missing,' Alec replied tartly. His back and legs ached and the wooden chair he sat in was uncomfortable.

'That's so,' Bezener agreed. He dug around in his teeth some more with the pick.

Alec shifted stiffly in his seat. 'I'm going tae the mine tomorrow, to talk tae the people who knew Haylock and Ford. I need to know if they were buddies.'

Bezener took the pick from his mouth and used it to comb through his moustache as he spoke. 'Mine's 'bout five miles outta town, but I guess that won't bother you none. It'll be a doddle after how far you done rode today.'

'Five miles is no distance,' Alec agreed, looking at the heavy man slouched back in his chair. He rose, suppressing a wince as his muscles protested.

Bezener was alert enough to notice his discomfort. 'Say, why don't you try a soak in one of the hot mineral springs? Folks come from all over to Ouray's springs,' he added proudly.

'I'm here on business, not pleasure,' Alec pointed out.

All the same, later that evening, he was floating contentedly in one of the nine hot springs in the town. It made sense, he told himself, because he needed to keep fit and well for his job. Alec sighed, and relaxed in the soothing waters.

CHAPTER TWELVE

Alec was up early the next morning, intending to make his call at the Pretty Boy mine and ride back to Montrose the same day. The air was fresh and invigorating as he left the town behind. His hired horse stepped out well, ears pricked, as they returned along the valley, before turning off the main trail in search of the mine. It wasn't hard to find: the trail was well worn and Alec only had to follow the sound of the machinery that pounded the ore and processed the metal. Smoke rose from the chimneys of the sprawling buildings into the blue sky.

Alec hitched his horse, and entered the office building, sited a short distance from the mills. A lanky young man sat behind the desk, busying himself organizing stacks of papers. His shirt, vest and tie were clean and tidy, but the jacket of his suit hung informally from the back of his chair. He looked up as Alec entered, and smiled, displaying a gap where one front tooth was missing.

'Good morning,' the clerk said brightly, waving to the chair in front of his desk. 'How may I help you, Sheriff?'

'It's Deputy US Marshal Lawson,' Alec corrected gently. Outside of his own county, he wore his deputy marshal badge in place of his sheriff badge, but the young man clearly didn't know the difference.

'Oh.' The young man flushed with embarrassment and dropped the pencil he'd been holding. He scrabbled about and picked it up again, while Alec suppressed a grin. 'You wrote to us about poor Haylock, didn't you? I'm Burton, by the way.'

Alec recognized Burton's accent as from New England, and educated.

'Pleased tae meet ye, Burton,' Alec replied. 'I was most grateful for the help ye gave me in identifying Haylock. I'm hoping ye can help some more.'

'Oh certainly, if I can,' Burton said with enthusiasm. 'It was such a relief to learn that Haylock had been murdered. Oh!' He flushed red and knocked over a pile of papers in his confusion. 'I didn't mean that the way it sounded!' He began scrabbling the pile of papers together. 'What I meant was that it was a relief to know what had happened to him, after he just vanished. I'm not pleased that he was killed. It's that I was glad to know what had happened, even though it was terrible.'

Alec cut off the young man's flustered burbling. 'I know what ye meant,' he said kindly and kept his face admirably straight as Burton covered his confusion by arranging the papers again.

'I understand that Haylock was reported missing tae Sheriff Bezener,' Alec said. 'Did Haylock tell anyone here about his plans, where he was going?'

'He told Brodie, he's the other assayist we employ, that he was going to look at some ore that Ford had found. He was pretty sure it would be good stuff, because Ford discovered the Pretty Boy lode. He told Brodie not to tell anyone what he was doing, and wouldn't say where he was going, because of keeping the strike secret, of course.'

'Did he say why Ford couldn't just bring a wee sample of the ore back to the mine to be tested?' Alec asked.

Burton's eyes widened. 'I never thought about that! It does seem rather peculiar. Ford could have just brought the ore back for testing without telling anyone where he found it.'

Alec thought for a moment. He was pretty certain that Ford had taken Haylock out on to Morpeth's land in order to murder him and frame Morpeth, but he wanted to know if there was any reason why Ford had chosen Haylock over Brodie.

'How well did Ford and Haylock get on?' Alec asked.

'Well, I know they played cards together,' Burton said, picking up his pencil again and twiddling it between his fingers. 'Haylock won a couple of hundred dollars off Ford a couple of weeks back. Ford was pretty sore about it. He kept saying how his cards had been bad, and he'd just had no luck.'

'He still kept betting, though,' Alec remarked.

Burton nodded. 'Ford always blames the cards when he loses. I don't play against him but he complains a lot about stuff. He owns half this mine but still reckons life owes him something.' He halted awkwardly, aware he was bad-mouthing his boss.

That comment confirmed Alec's opinion of Ford – an unsatisfied man who preferred to blame others for his problems, while seeking sympathy for them.

'Have ye heard from Ford since Haylock's death?' he asked.

Burton began rummaging in the piles of paper. 'He's sent a couple of letters. He said he'd gone to Lucasville for business, and been delayed there. I don't know what else was in them; it was about the mine.'

'Did he say anything about Haylock?'

Burton frowned. 'No, he didn't. He can't have: I'd heard nothing about it until you contacted us.' He looked at Alec, confused. 'But Haylock rode out to look at ore with Ford. Did they split up? Is that why Ford didn't know about Haylock being killed?'

'Ford knew,' Alec said grimly. 'He's the one who reported the murder.'

'Oh!' Burton dropped a hand on to a pile of papers, which promptly scattered across his desk. He didn't seem to notice. 'I'm sure he can't have mentioned it in his letters. We'd have been told. How odd.'

'There seems tae be a few things Ford hasna' told people,' Alec commented drily. He remembered another thing he wanted to ask. 'D'ye know what

Ford's like wi' horses? Is he interested in racing them?'

Burton grinned, showing the missing tooth. 'Last time anyone organized a horse race in Ouray, Ford lost fifty dollars. He claimed the races were rigged, but it was his fault; he had a real knack for picking the donkeys. He swore blind he'd never bet on a horse again.'

Alec grinned too, and rose. 'Thank ye very much for your time. You've been verra helpful.'

'I'm glad to help,' Burton responded.

They exchanged farewells and Alec left the office. He checked over his hired horse once more, then swung himself into the saddle and set off on the long journey back to Lucasville.

Alec finally stumbled back into the law building in Lucasville around half past nine in the morning, two days later. He was unshaven, heavy-eyed and unkempt. There was a lingering smell of coffee and bacon in the living quarters but although he was hungry, Alec was far too tired to eat.

Karl entered from the office and looked at him with some concern. 'We expected you back during the night.'

Alec dropped his leather bag on the floor. 'There was a landslide on the tracks twenty miles east of Gunnison.' He raised his arms and stretched, feeling joints pop in his spine. 'It delayed us two hours. I missed ma connection in Denver and spent four hours trying tae sleep on a chair in the waiting room while other trains kept whistling and waking me up.' He broke off for a face-splitting yawn.

'Well, there's nothing much to report from here,' Karl said. He moved to pick up the bag. 'Go sleep. You'll be no use for anything until you've had a decent rest.'

Alec didn't bother arguing, he merely followed Karl to the stairs.

It was the urgent need to urinate that finally woke Alec up. He fumbled his way out of the blankets, found the chamber pot under the bed and relieved himself, blinking sleepily at the dimly lit room. When he was done, he made his way rather stiffly to the window and opened the curtains a little way. It was going dark outside and golden light was showing from other windows in the street. Yawning and stretching, Alec thought longingly of the hot spa at Ouray. He dressed, relishing the clean clothes, and made his way down-stairs.

The other three lawmen were gathered in the back room. Karl was in his leather-covered chair, reading a book; Ethan and Sam were at the table, trading insults over a game of chequers. None of them noticed Alec arriving in his slippers. Alec paused in the doorway, grinned, then took a deep breath.

'Attention!'

The barked order had a startling effect on the room. Karl instinctively leapt to his feet and straight-ened into a military pose. Ethan stood up so fast his chair fell over and Sam knocked over the pile of cap-tured pieces he'd been stacking on the table before scrambling to his feet. Alec laughed as all three glared at him and began to relax.

'Boss, you've got a mean sense of humour,' Ethan complained before picking up his chair.

Still chuckling, Alec made his way into the room. 'It gets meaner when I need coffee.'

Ethan took the hint and moved over to the stove. His arm had healed well while Alec had been away, though he still kept it in a sling from time to time.

Karl came across and joined Alec in sitting at the table with Sam. Alec glanced at the clock on the wall; he'd slept for about twelve hours and it was after 9 p.m.

'Ye should ha' woken me earlier,' he said. 'I'll be awake half the night now.'

'You were exhausted,' Karl said. 'You'll get back to sleep sooner than you think, wake up late tomorrow and be fully recovered. It's better for you to miss a day and a half and be fully recovered, than to be out and still half-asleep if something happens.'

Alec glared at Karl but it was more for form than actual disapproval; he was used to giving orders, not to being taken charge of, but appreciated his friend's concern. The sound of a pan being clattered on to the stove was a welcome distraction.

'Figured you'd want something to go with the coffee,' Ethan said, dropping lard into the frying pan. 'Bacon and eggs?'

'Aye, thank ye,' Alec answered. 'How have things been here?' he asked Karl.

'Nothing very exciting. Ford came in to ask if you'd

133

arrested Morpeth yet. I told him you were away on other business.' Karl summarized the last few days' other events while the meal was cooked, with a few interjections from Sam and Ethan.

Alec's stomach was rumbling by the time the food was served and he ate hungrily before sitting back with a satisfied sigh. Sam cleared the plate away and they all settled in their armchairs for Alec to tell his news.

'As I thought, Ford's been telling us a pack of lies,' he said with disgust. Even just speaking about the man made Alec want to recoil. 'He lost money at cards to Haylock and grumbled about it, then asked him, instead o' the mine's other assayist, to ride out with him to look at some ore he'd found. He could ha' brought the ore tae the mine tae have it tested, but he took Haylock out on to Morpeth's land.'

'Did he ever do any horse training?' Sam asked.

Alec shook his head, smiling. 'It seems he couldn't pick a good horse if it had a laurel wreath hung round its neck and its owner was holding a big, gold trophy.'

'So what are you going to do, boss?' Sam asked.

'Arrest him for Haylock's murder,' Alec said with satisfaction. He glanced at the clock ticking on the shelf. 'In the morning,' he added.

'Have you got enough evidence to charge him?' Karl asked.

'I can show that he's told me a pack o' lies,' Alec replied. 'And that by losing money to Haylock at cards, he had reason tae be willing to kill him in order to frame Morpeth.' He looked at Ethan. 'I want tae find a prospector tomorrow and look for gold ore on Morpeth's land. If we can show there is gold there, and mebbe someone had already been looking for it, that will help ma theory.'

Ethan nodded. 'Good thinking.'

'Ford lied about what he'd been doing and about how Haylock was killed. If we can put that together with him having a reason to dislike Haylock and for wanting Morpeth off his land, I reckon we can convince a jury,' Alec said confidently.

'I figure you're right,' Sam said. He stood up. 'Who's for a game of poker?'

It was mid-morning before Alec set out, accompanied by Ethan, to arrest Ford at his hotel. He looked in at the parlour, but there was no sign of the geologist, so Alec went to the reception desk and introduced himself.

'I'm looking for Frank Ford.'

The man behind the desk shook his head. 'I'm afraid you just missed him, Sheriff. He done checked out just a few minutes ago.'

'Checked out?' Alec repeated. 'Bags and all?'

The clerk nodded. 'Sure, he settled up and quit his room here.' He made a face. 'Wanted to know if one of the bellhops would tote his things down to the railroad station for him, for free if you please, 'cause he'd been staying here a while.'

'Right, thank you,' Alec added as he spun and hurried away, Ethan following.

They burst out into the warm sunshine. The sidewalks were busy, so Alec jumped down the steps into the street and started running, dodging between wagons.

'Why's he upped and left now?' Ethan asked as they ran.

'Must have got spooked yesterday when he learnt I was away. Could ha' asked at the station an' found I'd gone towards Ouray,' Alec answered, passing a buckboard.

A few minutes later they arrived at Lucasville's railroad station, slightly out of breath. Wagons rumbled back and forth from the goods depot and buggies clustered around, waiting on the hope of picking up arriving passengers. There was a smell of hot oil and metal that was even stronger than the smell of men and horses. Alec pushed his way through the milling people, regretting his lack of height as he tried to see Ford. Ethan was a couple of inches taller; he spotted Ford first.

'There!' he exclaimed, pointing. 'In line at the booking window.'

'Move aside!' Alec bellowed the order at the people in front of him.

As they parted in obedience to the authority in his voice, Ford turned and saw the lawmen approaching. He glanced about, then took off at a run, clutching a carpetbag. Alec and Ethan gave chase. Alec shouted an order to stop, but Ford kept running, leaping over the nearest set of rails. He swerved and headed for a train that was just beginning to move. Alec drew his pistol and fired after him, missing. Ford dropped the carpetbag and accelerated. Ethan and Alec both fired again as Ford closed with the last boxcar of the departing train.

'Don't shoot! Don't shoot!' The plea was frantic as a railroad man sprinted out from the goods yard. 'There's naphtha oil in that car!'

Alec felt a surge of horror: naphtha was flammable, like kerosene, and a bullet might be enough to set it off. He holstered his gun again, as Ethan overtook him. As fast as they ran, Ford had too much of a lead. He grabbed for the ladder at the end of a goods car and swung himself on to it, scrambling up as the train gathered speed. In just a few more strides, Alec realized that he and Ethan couldn't catch up; he dropped into a jog for a few strides, then a walk as the railroad man caught up with them.

'Where's that train going?' Alec gasped. Ford had made it on to the roof and was only just visible as he lay flat.

'Lyons, Dronfield, Narrow and Estes Park,' the man replied.

'When's the next train going that way?'

'It ain't but fifty minutes.'

Alec swore. 'He'll get too far ahead of us.'

The railroad man shook his head. 'Next train's the express. Goods train pulls into a siding at Narrow to unload and let the express come past. Express reaches Narrow 'bout twenty minutes later, God willing an' the creek don't rise.'

Alec spun, full of energy again. 'Ethan, get back to the office and fetch the others. I'm going to speak to Webb and get us places on the express.'

Ethan nodded and ran back into the town, while Alec made for the office of the owner of the railroad company.

CHAPTER THIRTEEN

Ethan pressed his head against the window to look out of the express car.

'Are we there yet?' Sam asked, in the irrepressible tones of a child, bouncing in his seat beside Ethan.

Alec suppressed the urge to grin at Ethan's pained expression. 'We should be in Dronfield in a couple of minutes,' he said. 'The train's going tae stop for water, so we'd best get off and ask around, in case anyone's seen Ford leaving the goods train.'

Sure enough, a couple of minutes later the train halted with a whistle and billow of steam at the little town in the mountains. The lawmen got off and asked questions of the people around the station but no one resembling Ford's description had been seen travelling on or leaving the goods train. Alec went and spoke to the locomotive engineer who was supervising the watering and refuelling of his engine.

'The engineer says it will be a few minutes before we leave,' Alec told his deputies. 'I'm going to telegraph the marshal at Narrow an' ask him tae look out for Ford.'

'We'll keep our eyes open here,' Karl promised. 'Just in case he did slip off.'

Alec nodded, and made his way to the telegraph office, which was attached to the end of the depot building.

Inside, the telegraph operator was busy at the key. As Alec waited, he found himself listening to the rapid bursts of sound from the telegraph machine. He'd learnt to use one whilst in the Army and couldn't help but try to interpret the signals coming through. He was out of practice, but after a minute or so, he began to pick out the groups that made up certain letters. He drew the letters in the air, trying to visualize them and form words. The movement attracted the attention of the operator, who glanced at him briefly.

When the message was taken and written neatly on a form, Alec stepped closer to dictate the message he wanted to send. The operator, who looked to be no older than about seventeen, grinned.

'I reckon you could send it yourself,' he said, gesturing to the key.

Alec shook his head. 'It's been a while an' I never was a regular operator. Be quicker if you do it.' He dictated his message to the sheriff at Narrow and listened to the brisk click of the key as it was sent.

Leaning back, the young operator looked up at him. 'I'd be plumb grateful if you'd do me a favour, Sheriff. I'm not expecting any messages about the trains coming through soon, an' I really have to go piss. Could you sit by the key, just in case something does come through?'

'I don't swear as I'd catch everything,' Alec said hesitantly.

'It'd be better than no one being here,' pleaded the youth. 'I really gotta go.'

The restless way he moved in his seat convinced Alec. 'All right.'

'Thanks!' The operator was out of his seat faster than a startled jackrabbit.

Alec sat down in his place and looked at the key, notepad and pencil all set out. He'd barely had time to take it in when the key started chattering. Alec swore and grabbed for notepad and pencil, writing down letters as he caught them. He very quickly realized that he'd never keep up enough for his notes to make sense and so pressed down his own key to interrupt. As he held it down, he thought of what he wanted to send, and the Morse letters started forming themselves in his mind. Alec began tapping the key, hesitantly at first, but soon more confidently.

STOP OPERATOR AWAY REPEAT SLOWLY END

Taking up the pencil, he began writing again as the letters came though once more. The other operator didn't query him but simply spilled out his message. Alec had to take a guess at some of the letters, working them out from context. The message was from Narrows. Concentrating on each letter, Alec barely had time to take in the words they formed, let alone

141

complete sentences, but he caught enough for a growing sense of horror to settle in his stomach. Only when the sender stopped could he read the whole message.

As he did, the operator returned. 'What's happened?' he asked, looking guilty.

Alec rose abruptly. 'Get on to Narrow and get the operator to repeat the message he just sent, to confirm I got it right.' With that, Alec sprinted from the office.

His abrupt arrival on the platform drew the attention of his deputies, who hurried towards him. Alec explained things fast, but quietly.

'I just got word from Narrow. Two goods cars from the end of the freight train have been detached and are rolling back towards us.'

'The one full of naphtha?' Ethan asked.

Alec nodded. 'The other's got a load of Giant's powder.' Giant's powder was a type of explosive.

'I bet it was Ford,' Sam said, his usually merry face now icily cold. 'He must have guessed we'd follow him.'

'We'll worry about the culprit later,' Alec said. 'Ethan, you're lookout; find a horse and ride up the line a wee way. Warn us as soon as those wagons come into sight.'

'Right.' Ethan spun and raced off.

Alec looked at his other two deputies. 'There's no point trying tae back the express up. It can't outrun the goods cars back to Lucasville, and even if it did, they'd hit it there.'

'Can't we just back it up out of Dronfield?' Karl asked.

Alec looked at the gently steaming locomotive, still being fed by the water tower. It wasn't due to move for at least a couple more minutes. He shook his head.

'Pressure's too low tae move now. You start evacuating the passengers, I'll go tell the engineer tae start raising steam.'

The lawmen separated, heading to their separate tasks. As Alec approached the engineer, the telegraph operator came racing up, waving a telegram form.

'It's going to be a disaster!' the young man yelled.

Everyone in earshot turned to him, and Alec could hear them asking anxious questions of one another. He fixed the young man with a fierce glare.

'Quiet now! We dinna want tae be starting a panic.' He turned to the engineer. 'We need tae get everyone off this train as fast as possible, then back it out of town if we can. Boxcars from the freight train at Narrow are rolling loose back down the track towards us. They're loaded with explosives. Get that water tower unhitched and start raising steam.'

The engineer stared at Alec, wide-eyed for a moment, then sprinted for his locomotive, yelling orders to his fireman.

Alec turned to the telegraph operator. 'Go to the buildings nearest the station and start banging on doors. Tell folks tae clear out tae the other side of town.'

'Yessir!' Still clutching his telegram form, the young man sprinted away.

Alec turned and took a few moments to study the train. It had seven passenger cars, a boxcar of horses and the caboose. Already people were descending the steps at either end of the first two cars, clutching bags and packages. They gathered in nervous groups, voices raised anxiously. Alec strode towards the nearest cluster.

'I'm Sheriff Lawson. Please, all leave the station and go to the far end of the street.' One or two started to move. Alec swept his gaze across the others. 'You're in danger here,' he said bluntly. 'Get clear now.'

Most of them began to move. A brawny young man with the tan of a farmer turned back towards the train. 'I got a sack of seed corn on board.' Others started to turn back too.

Alec grabbed the young man and spun him around, moving faster than the surprised man could react. 'Ye can't plant seed corn if you're dead or maimed,' he snapped. 'You make me waste any more time and I'll pick up any bits of you that survive and throw them in jail.'

The young farmer didn't argue any more but joined the rest of the passengers as they began to hurry away.

Alec spotted the station agent and called him over as he hurried towards the second group of passengers clustering around the rear door of the car.

'Tom told me about the loose cars,' the agent said. He was wide-eyed with anxiety but seemed to be holding himself together.

'Organize the folks getting off the train,' Alec ordered. 'Get them moving as far away as possible.

Does the town have a fire brigade?'

The station agent shook his head. 'We do have a drill for fires, though.'

'Good. Send someone to get water ready and fix up a bucket line.'

As the agent called for Tom, the telegraph operator, Alec saw Karl jump down the steps from the first passenger car. Sam was visible in the second.

'All out,' Karl called.

'Good work. Get more of these people moving; I'll clear the third car.'

Already, a few passengers were climbing out of the other cars and looking around in a bewildered manner. The conductor was reassuring the ones nearer the back and urging them to board the train. Alec sprinted to him.

'We hafta get them off,' he said.

The tall conductor looked down at him. 'Who the hell are you?'

'Sheriff Lawson,' Alec snapped, fixing the conductor with a glare. 'There's goods cars loaded with explosives rolling back down the track from Narrow.'

The conductor's eyes widened in panic as he glanced towards the steaming locomotive at the head of the train.

'Get people off and away,' Alec ordered. 'Don't let them panic.'

The conductor nodded, and swung himself on board the nearest car, giving instructions in a tightly controlled voice.

Karl came up to Alec at a brisk trot. 'First car is

clear,' he reported.

'Good; clear the third, I'll do the fourth.'

Alec raced to the fourth car and the handful of people gathered around the nearest door.

'What's going on?' a bald-headed man asked.

'The train hasta' be evacuated now,' Alec said, loud enough for all the people around to hear. 'There's danger of an explosion. Leave the train and take yourselves to the far end o' the street. Get well clear.' He pointed to the street beyond the station.

The people around started moving, some with evident panic. A woman on the steps turned and called to those still inside the car before starting to climb down. Alec helped her down the last couple of steps, then climbed up himself.

'Sheriff Lawson. Let me on board!' The authority in his voice cleared a way for him.

Alec pushed into the vestibule at the end of the car and faced the aisle. Already, people were standing, gathering bags and children, and starting to make their way out. Others were arguing with one another, either staying in place or shoving into the aisle.

'Attention!' Alec bellowed, in the voice that was obeyed immediately across parade ground or battlefield. The passengers stopped milling and a brief hush fell. 'I'm Sheriff Lawson. I'm ordering everyone tae leave this train now. Take only small bags and move quietly. Dinna push anyone, there's enough time. When ye're off the train, leave the station and make for the other end of the road. Get clear of the station. Now move, and help one another if ye can.'

Alec watched as the passengers began evacuating from the train. As they filled the aisle and began to filter past him, he saw a large man, probably a miner, shove past a woman carrying a child, sending her staggering into an empty seat. Alec's pistol was out and pointed at the miner in a moment.

'You!'

The miner froze, and looked about uncertainly.

'You with the red necktie,' Alec clarified. 'Move aside intae that empty seat.' He indicated one on the other side. 'Ye can wait there until everyone else is out of the way. You'll be last off but me.'

Someone helped the woman up as passengers kept moving. When there were no more behind the miner, Alec gestured for him to join the end of the line. One after another, people clutching bags and babies climbed down the steps and hurried away, marshalled by the station staff. The miner silently passed Alec and climbed down. Alec holstered his pistol and followed.

When he was on the ground again, he found that Sam was clearing the fifth car and the conductor had moved to the sixth. That left only the caboose and the horse box. Even as he considered the horse box, Alec heard the sound of a galloping horse approaching, and Ethan calling his name.

'Alec! Two, three minutes!'

Alec turned to the people nearby. 'Pick the children up and run. Get as far away as you can,' he ordered. A quick gesture was enough to tell Ethan to accompany them. 'You, you, an' you, come with me.' He picked out the three burliest men he could see and ran for the horse car.

There would be no time to unload all the horses, and he could hear from stamping and restless snorts that they had picked up on the disturbance outside and were upset.

'I'll release the car and we'll roll it back away,' he explained to the men with him. 'We can mebbe save them from the impact.'

As the men took up positions to push, Alec squeezed between the last passenger car and the horse box. For a moment he hesitated, sick with fear. When working in a railroad yard, he'd seen men crushed to death between cars when they came together suddenly. The wooden bumpers at the ends of the cars crushed them as if in a vice. The cars were joined by a metal link, shaped like a large version of a link in a chain. The ends were inserted into sockets at the end of each car, and held in place with long metal spikes known as pins. The sockets on these two cars were at different heights, and whoever had coupled the train together had been forced to use a bent, gooseneck link. It wasn't quite the right size, however, and the pins were jammed in at an awkward angle.

Alec swore, and started to pull at the higher pin. He wriggled it to try and work it at a better angle, all the time aware of his dangerous position between the cars. Metal scraped but the pin yielded a bare inch. Gritting his teeth, Alec pulled again but he didn't have the physical strength to shift it.

'Here.' Karl suddenly appeared on the other side of the coupling, holding a lump hammer he'd got from somewhere. Bracing himself, he swung the hammer against the pin from beneath. It shot up, and Alec wrestled with it as Karl prepared for another swing. At the second blow, it popped out. Alec just let it fall, not noticing the skin scraped from the palm of his hands. He turned and placed his shoulder against the back of the horse box, as Karl did the same on the other side.

'Ready? Push!'

With the other men, Alec applied his weight and strength to the wagons. Nothing seemed to happen at first, then he felt them begin to move.

'They're going!' someone yelled.

As the dead weight got under way, the wagons became easier to move. The gap opened from a couple of feet to six feet to ten feet. Then the loco-motive whistle blew shrilly.

'Get clear!' Alec bellowed the order as he dived sideways. Barely keeping his balance, he sprinted away from the tracks. A few seconds later, he heard the crash as the free-running goods wagons hit the sta-tionary locomotive. The passenger cars rattled together, the sound almost drowned by screams. As Alec looked, he saw the wooden freight cars crum-pling as they slammed against the locomotive and one another. Naphtha oil spilt from the first car and promptly caught fire in the heat from the locomotive. Scarce moments seemed to pass before flames were licking at the shattered remains of the freight car.

CHAPTER FOURTEEN

The next few minutes passed in a blur of smoke and fire. They battled valiantly, but the bucket chain wasn't enough to put the fire out, or to adequately dampen the car containing Giant's powder. As the first flames roared up on the powder car, Alec ordered everyone to run. He raced away, Karl beside him. In spite of the smoke and sweat, Karl still looked dignified: Alec felt anything but. They made it some three hundred yards away before the powder exploded.

The blast was still enough to knock Alec off his feet. He hit the ground hard, rolled twice and stayed down, covering his head with his arms. Dirt and debris landed on and around him. The sound had almost deafened him, but he could still hear crashes and screams. Only when the muffled noises died down did he lift his head and painfully sit upright. For the first few moments, all he did was to stare around in shock. Over half the town had vanished: buildings were reduced to heaps of broken lumber. A twisted piece of railroad track lay just a few feet from his side. Flames and black smoke still rose from a massive crater where the train had once been. As he climbed stiffly to his feet, Alec saw other people beginning to move.

Karl was beside him, looking as shaken as Alec felt. Alec looked around hastily and was relieved to see Sam getting to his feet a short distance away, and Ethan with the groups of dazed people gathered before the buildings left at the end of the street. After the first, shocked silence, the air began to fill with the sounds of people calling for help, sobbing, and the crying of children.

'Where do we start?' Karl asked in dazed tones, and rather too loudly.

The words were still rather muffled to Alec after the blast. He drew a deep breath, and also spoke loudly over the ringing in his ears. 'Take Sam and join Ethan. Organize men to searching for the injured.' As he started to make decisions, his mind seemed to clear and the shakiness vanished under the need to help others. 'Find a schoolroom or saloon where the women and bairns can go. If there's women without children, or older girls, set them tae fetching blankets from houses, and heating water. Find anyone who can nurse tha injured.'

'Yes, sir.' Karl started to turn, then stopped. 'What about you?' He pointed at Alec to clarify what he meant.

'I need to check down there,' Alec shook his head, winced, then pointed to the crater.

Karl hesitated for a moment, then nodded and went to fulfil his designated tasks.

As Alec moved, the stiffness eased somewhat. He reached the edge of the crater, which was almost forty feet across. The mangled wreck of the locomotive, tender and cars were still burning at the centre. The wreckage of the station building was strewn about, barely recognizable as such. Amongst the debris was the body of the telegraph operator. Alec didn't need to get close to see that the man was dead: he lay sprawled in his own blood, shards of window glass piercing his body. His right hand was still clutching a telegram form, somehow undamaged. Alec scrambled carefully down the slope to the body, and pried the form from the dead man's hand. He read it in a quick glance, then scrabbled his way out of the pit at speed.

A shout and some waving brought his deputies running to meet him in the middle of the devastated town.

'What is it, boss?' Sam got the question out first.

Alec waved the telegraph form at them. 'Ford got off the train at Narrow.' He modified his shouting a little as he realized the deafness was beginning to wear off. 'He stole a horse and was seen riding south-west along Rock Creek. Ford's bound tae come out on the Middle Saint Vrain.' Alec gestured at the valley leading off to their west. 'The head of Rock Creek valley is the other side of the ridge from that one. It'll be more level going along there; I can catch up with him about when he crosses the ridge. I'll need that horse you had,' he said to Ethan.

'Yo.' Ethan answered in the cavalry way and sprinted off to fetch the borrowed mount.

'We'll need horses too,' Sam said, turning.

'No,' Alec ordered. 'You three need tae stay here and take care of these people. Ah can take care o' Ford by myself,' he added coldly.

Sam and Karl knew better than to argue with him when he looked that way.

'Take care,' was all Karl said, though his eyes expressed more.

'Ford is the one who needs tae tek care,' Alec replied simply.

Ethan's borrowed horse was a plain brown, small and sturdy but with an intelligent look in its eyes. Alec vaulted into the saddle and set off at a steady jog, adjusting the stirrups as he rode. He gave the brown a pat on the neck and spoke to it as they headed along the valley out of town.

'I dinna know your name, but we got an important job tae do.'

The brown flicked its ears back towards him as he spoke. Its jog was steady and comfortable, and Alec got the impression it could keep up the pace for hours. He needed to go faster, though, but knew better than to let his impatience get the better of him. After the first mile, he pushed the horse into a lope, and alternated between the two paces. At about four miles, they had to cross the river. Alec stopped, letting the horse have a short drink, while he had a drink himself. Then he was back in the saddle for the last mile to where he thought Ford would most likely be entering this valley.

There was only one viable way out of the valley Ford had fled along. As soon as he saw the pass, Alec moved his mount to the opposite side of the valley he was following, climbing the side a short way to get amongst the trees. He could hear the distant thunder of processing at a mine he'd passed, but the sound was muffled by the trees. His knew his own hearing had returned now, as he could hear the scolding of a grey jay from somewhere nearby. Alec found a spot where he could see out without being too obvious himself, and where he could work out a route back to the valley floor, and waited.

He had to wait longer than he expected. As far as he could remember, Ford's journey was shorter, and he'd set off first, but was mostly uphill. Alec had been hoping to get to the head of the Rock Creek valley before Ford did, but it was possible that Ford had beaten him, crossed the ridge, and had already ridden off up the Saint Vrain valley that Alec was now waiting in. Alec watched the other side of the valley eagerly, trying not to fidget and fret as the minutes passed. If Ford had reached this point first, he would be getting further and further away now. Alec thought of the dead telegraph operator, and the devastated town, and his impatience to catch Ford grew. The brown stretched its neck to snatch a mouthful of thimbleberry leaves and Alec was severely tempted to jerk on the reins to keep it still. He forced himself to stay quiet as he waited, all the time worried that he'd misjudged things.

At last, his patience was rewarded. Ford came into view at the top of the dividing ridge, keeping a tight rein on his horse as it picked its way down the slope into Alec's valley. Closing his legs against its sides, Alec turned his horse down the slope. Unlike Ford, Alec sat forward in his saddle, keeping himself better balanced and able to guide the horse through the trees. He was still in full control as the brown jumped the last few feet and landed on the valley floor at a lope.

Ford was still concentrating on his horse, and didn't look up. Alec gathered his horse neatly and sent it forward. He drew his gun as they reached the shallow river and splashed through it. Ford heard them, and looked up suddenly.

'Halt and surrender!' Alec commanded, as the brown bounded on to the shore.

Ford panicked. He glanced about, then drew his own gun while urging his horse on faster. He fired, but it was a wild shot from an erratically moving horse, and missed.

Alec pulled his own horse to a halt and gave Ford a second chance, unwilling to kill unnecessarily.

'Drop the gun and surrender,' he ordered.

This time, Ford tried to aim. Alec couldn't hear or see the bullet, but the brown flinched, so he knew it must have come closer.

'It wasn't my fault!' Ford yelled, still pointing his

gun roughly in Alec's direction as his horse bounded to the valley floor. 'You forced me to unhook the cars.'

Alec's temper flared at the whining accusation. 'No one forced ye tae do anything.' He dug his heels into the brown's sides and sent it forward.

Ford was out of balance with his horse. He lurched in the saddle as it landed, which saved him from Alec's first shot. He returned fire, causing the brown to spook. Alec stayed in place, firmly controlling the horse with legs and reins. They fired at almost the same time. Ford cried out and grabbed for his saddle horn with his left hand as blood blossomed on that shoulder. He kept hold of his gun, though, and tried to cock it. Alec wasn't taking any more risks: he'd given Ford a fair chance to surrender, and the chance had been ignored. Alec took a couple of moments to aim, and fired again.

This bullet hit Ford full in the chest, knocking him back to slide off his horse. The stolen horse shied away, frightened. Alec nudged his own forward and caught its reins, keeping his eyes on Ford as much as possible. Ford lay in the grass, moaning and pleading for help for a few breaths. By the time Alec had caught the horse, Ford was silent and still.

Alec watched him for a few moments, giving himself and the horses time to calm down. Dismounting, he walked over to Ford, gun in hand, and studied the body. Satisfied that Ford was dead, he holstered his pistol, and knelt to check and search the body.

*

Sam whistled as he looked at Ford's bankbook, back in the office in Lucasville the following morning. 'He sure had a heap of money, didn't he?'

The four of them were gathered around the large desk in his private office. Alec had glanced through the bankbook, and a notebook, which he now held.

'Is there enough left to rebuild Dronfield and pay the medical bills?' Karl asked.

Alec had returned to the devastated town with Ford's body to find his deputies helping deal with the aftermath of the train explosion. Thanks to their work in evacuating people, only three had been killed outright, and twelve badly injured. Many more had suffered shock, scrapes and bruises, but people had rallied together, under the leadership of the lawmen, to help one another. Alec and his deputies had arrived back in Lucasville in the dark, exhausted from their labours.

'Ford's money will go to the state,' Alec pointed out, 'but a relief fund's already been set up to help the victims. I was told about it first thing.'

There were sounds of approval from around the desk.

'We know as it was Ford who released those goods cars,' Sam drawled. 'We done got a witness in Narrow saw him fiddling with the cars, though didn't know as he wasn't with the railroad. I don't see how we're ever goin' to know for sure if it was Ford who killed Haylock.'

'I reckon we've got pretty good evidence.' Alec laid the pocketbook on the table, along with a hand-drawn map he'd found folded up inside it. 'Can you see where this is?' he asked, indicating an area of the map.

His deputies studied the piece of paper.

'Those look like rivers,' Karl said. 'Coming together like that, assuming the map's local, I'd guess that one's the Little Thompson, and that's the South Saint Vrain.' Alec nodded so he continued. 'In that case, this area marked with the dotted line must be Morpeth's land.'

'You're right,' Alec said. 'See the letters marking spots on Morpeth's land? There's letters that match them in this notebook, under this heading Box M. . . .'

'Morpeth's brand,' Ethan put in.

'Right, and beside each letter is an amount in dollars per tonne, and either S or G.'

'The value of the ore found at each spot, and the metal, gold or silver.' Karl said. 'Ford was a geologist; he found the ore. Then when he had a couple of likely spots, he brought in Haylock to assay each one, so he could see if they were worth mining.'

Alec nodded agreement. 'There's gold worth fifty dollars a tonne, and silver between thirty and a hundred and twenty.'

Sam whistled. 'Ford sure wouldn't want anyone else knowing there was ore that valuable on Morpeth's land.'

'But first he had to get Morpeth off the land,' Ethan pointed out. 'I'll bet it was like you guessed, Alec. If he done killed Morpeth and Haylock, we might have found out who was behind one or both murders. Instead, Ford killed Haylock to silence him, then done accused Morpeth to get him charged, and preferably hanged, so he could buy Morpeth's land.' He shook his head. 'Cruel. Efficient, but cruel.'

'At least Alec here done saved the county the cost of a trial and a hanging,' Sam pointed out cheerfully.

'And saved us some paperwork,' Ethan said, looking cheerful for once.

'And Morpeth has a fortune under his land,' Karl added.

'Can't you think of some reason to arrest him, or confiscate his land, so as I can buy it?' Sam asked Alec plaintively.

Alec chuckled. 'Ye canna afford the land,' he said. 'And you'll never afford it if ye doan' earn some money by getting some work done. You and Ethan have some brands to go inspect, so get on with it.'

Sam and Ethan departed, grumbling. Karl had to leave to run an auction of a tax defaulter's goods. Alec was left alone in his office. He folded the map and put it back into the notebook, and put that and the bankbook into a drawer in his desk. Leaning back in his chair, he thought about Ford for a few minutes. Ford's callous behaviour niggled at him, irritating him. Annoyed at Ford, and at himself for thinking about him, Alec decided to think about something more pleasant. Miss Lily was the first thing that came to his mind. It seemed a long time since he had seen her. He wondered how she was getting on in her new life with the Browns.

He needed something refreshing and wholesome; a visit to the family home of the Browns would be just the thing. It was only natural that having asked the Browns to look after her, he should take an interest in Lily's progress. Smiling to himself, Alec left his office and went upstairs to brush his hair and smarten himself up before calling on the Browns, and Lily.